The Story Must Be Told

Seasons of the Story

by Brother Reid & Pastor Andrew

Artwork by Sishir Bommakanti
Cover art and book design by Brother Reid

The Story Must Be Told
Post Everything Productions
Copyright 2021

BY ALL ACCOUNTS, THIS BOOK SHOULD NOT EXIST

A Foreword to *Seasons of the Story*

Not unlike the Lost City of Atlantis or the state of Florida,[1] *Seasons of the Story* was believed to be a myth by scholars world- and space-wide. But thanks to over a century of cooperation among anthropologists, archaeologists, pre-collapse theologians, and a band of plucky robots, *Seasons of the Story* has been made whole once again. While we may never know if every Story has been recovered, my research team and I have attempted in earnest to publish this edition of *Seasons of the Story* as close to its original form as possible. What we present to you is an unadulterated and unabridged edition of *Seasons of the Story*, the first of its kind in nearly a millennium.

So, what *do* we know? We know to a near certainty that it

---

[1] While records cannot be verified, scholars posit that "Florida" was a province in the Empire of the United States, allegedly responsible for the fatal Gator Pox pandemic in the late 2000s.

was published in the early 2000s, and that it is a collection of spiritual texts from a now-extinct religion called "The Story." *Seasons of the Story*'s tone suggests it was written by two authors, perhaps high priests. We believe adherents of the Story referred to these men as Brother Reid and Pastor Andrew, and so we have attributed this book to them. Whether or not these men ever existed is up for debate, nor does it matter.

The reason we know so little about the Story's origins is because the Story isn't mentioned in historical documents until the mid 2300s. However, this shouldn't come as a surprise, as the 2000s through the 2300s span "The Second Dark Age." To further complicate matters, the most recent Story fragment is merely a reproduction that dates back all the way to 2522, and only in the past fifteen years did hyper-intelligent space apes begin piecing *Seasons of the Story* together into the finished product we have today.[2] For such an old text, it is very new to us.

In the relatively short time scholars have had to compare the recovered text of *Seasons of the Story* to archaeological excavations of devastated, abandoned cities from The Second Dark Age, we're beginning to think that the very publication of *Seasons of the Story* might be responsible for the global unrest that plummeted society into centuries-long pandemonium. From the subterranean rubble of these obliterated cities, anthropologists and archaeologists have discovered ancient graffiti[3] referencing the Story, as well as the remains of alleged holy sites, like

---

[2] Completing the text of *Seasons of the Story* fulfilled the final reparations obligations for the Federal Empire of Spatium Gorilla Mate, thus repaying their debt for international damages they caused in the Fourth Intergalactic Space War.

[3] On the walls of the ancient German Bundestag, an unknown person (or robot) scratched "Die Geschichte hat uns gut geschmiert," roughly translated to "The Story greased us good."

the Shrine of the Story in Toledo, Ohio.[4]

As it stands, it's taken nearly 700 years to gather the fragments we do have, both on Earth and in space. Placing the Story in a historical context could take even longer. Future editions of *Seasons of the Story* will be updated as research progresses.

But let us entertain this thought for just a moment: that the publication of *Seasons of the Story* caused a massive, destructive global event. This could mean that you, dear reader, are holding what might be the most dangerous book in the history of humanity.[5] Let us reiterate, this is just a theory. Until we find the second Rosetta Stone that might reboot the mysterious, so-called "Internet," we will never know the series of events as they unfolded. However, it's worth considering.

The few companion pieces to *Seasons of the Story* that we've found along the way tell a tale of Story adherents risking their lives to smuggle pieces of transcribed Stories across borders so that they might be shared with small Story communities across the world. Those who were caught were decried as rebels, imprisoned and sent to space jail.[6] One of the more remarkable accounts we've uncovered is that of Danthia Slurpminn.[7] When a firing squad armed with plasma rays took aim at her, she cried out, "Grease me up or plump me down!" before being reduced to subatomic particles. When this account was recently published

---

[4] Both human and canine remains are buried at this particular site and several others. Scientists hypothesize that wealthy Story adherents were buried with their dogs to take to the afterlife, believing dog bones could be used as currency.

[5] Followed closely by *Chicken Soup for the Teen Soul*, about which we know much.

[6] Although now we simply call it "jail."

[7] Danitha Slurpminn could be the far, distant relative of Grips "Chunky" Slurpminn, founder and CEO of the popular intergalactic casual family dining chain, "Chunky's Delights."

in *The Intergalactic Times*, a fledgling political party in the Netherlands proposed legislation to put "Grease me up or plump me down!" on its currency. The Story lives on.

Regarding its format, it's unclear why the original authors structured *Seasons of the Story* the way they did. Academia is divided on why it's titled *Seasons of the Story* in the first place. *Story*, yes, that much is clear. But the word *Seasons* has been lost to time. There are two prevailing theories. The first, and most likely, is that Seasons refers to a ceremony. In the book, four Seasons are mentioned: Recollection, Witness, Prophesy, and Revelation. Perhaps a formal sacrament was attached to each section when the Story was read or performed for the masses.[8] The history of theology supports this theory. A second, and less believable theory, is that *Seasons* refers to the climate of planet Earth in the 2000s, when it was originally published. Oft-dismissed pseudo-scientists maintain that, throughout the year, the world used to experience four specific weather patterns, ranging from cold, to mild, to hot, to cool. In this case, *Seasons* would be used in a poetic sense. However, as Earth has maintained a consistent temperature of 138° Farenheit for the past 700 years, this theory is hard to take seriously.

As for the Stories themselves, they are yours to discover, dear reader. Are they morality plays, or simply entertainment? Are they a reflection of what life might have been like in the 2000s, before people wore SmartJeans™? Could this book, perhaps, be an artifact of the world's only true religion? That question is for you to answer. In the opinion of this author, the answer is "Yes."

I'd like to thank my assistant, Krimb "Robo" Cyborgian, for all their hard work documenting my notes and keeping me

---

[8] From recovered sundials and humorous daily desk calendars, it's believed that the contemporary intergalactic holiday "Space Christmas" could be an appropriation of the Story holiday, "Greasegiving."

on track, through thick and thin. A thank you is in order for the eight hard-working, no-nonsense robots of Space Station 12, who I will thank by name: Robot 1, Robot 2, Robot 3, Robot 4, Robot 5, Robot 6, Robot 7, and of course, Robot 8. And finally, a dear thank you to my loving and patient husband, Crisp.

The Story Must Be Told.

- L.T. Taster V, Ph.D
Princeton University, Mars Campus

*-"Lil" Tad Taster V,
taken during his coma* [9]

---

9   Space coma.

CONTENTS

Recollection — 5

The Bear Musician 6
After the Attack 13
The Boys Open 26
Dick Dvorak Bowls a Perfect Game 33
The Passage of Memory 48

Witness — 67

The Pilot 68
The Bird That Learned About Weekends 74
Hot Pics Wedding Rings OK 84
Maps of the North 104
The Mathematics of Grocery Stores 121

Prophecy — 133

The First Photo of God 134
A Man for the Woman 151
The New Consciousness in Town 161
Fun Boy Limited Party Travel Number One 173
They Made a Strange Love 185

Revelation — 195

The Story of Revelation: The Revelation of Story 196

The Story Must Be Told

Seasons of the Story

Recollection

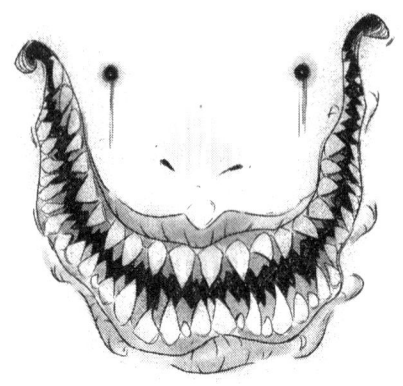

THE BEAR MUSICIAN

The 57th Story ⚓

Bruno hobbled off the ferry onto dry ground. He carried a small box with his only possessions: a pencil, naturalization documents, a pair of socks, and a faded picture of his mother. He limped away from the boat, set his box on the the dirt, and sat.

In the gutters, rotting food waste, horse shit, piss, and dead vermin floated in standing water. The overwhelming stench put a pause on his hunger and silenced the rattling between his bony ribs. Bruno's mouth went dry and his tongue swelled, heaving him forward to vomit. He retched without purchase.

It was morning and the city was buzzing. An exasperated traffic cop failed to direct coachmen. Carriages charged by with abandon. One took a corner too fast. It tilted on two wheels, hopped up a curb, and ran over the back legs of a stray dog. Whimpering, the dog crawled into a gutter and out of view. Outside a pub, two men with cartoonishly large hands swung

---

⚓ From: The Book of Aimless Sons and Thoughtful Boys.

at each other, delivering blow after blow, neither falling down. Prostitutes, woozy from drink, swayed on corners looking for an early morning john.

Typhus ravaged the ship two months into the journey. Most died. Bruno and his mother arrived on Ellis Island, hungry and dehydrated, among one fourth of the manifest who survived. While in mandatory quarantine, he laid in bed next to her as she coughed through the night. When he awoke, there was a mist of blood on her pillow. Her eyelids were open with a milky film over her once bright green eyes. She had seen Death and He had taken her. Three months later, the nearly fourteen-year-old Bruno sat at the tip of America's most infamous island, shaking with fear.

A group of women in maroon dresses approached Bruno with a slice of bread and a pamphlet covered in words he didn't understand, although he did recognize the Christian cross on the first page. As one of the women spoke to him in a strange language, he unfolded the pamphlet and used it as a napkin while he ate the bread. Furious at his sacrilege, the woman pulled the pamphlet and the bread from his hands, delivering a cracking slap across his cheekbone. His ears rang and his eyes swelled as she stormed away.

Bruno held his face and clenched his teeth as he waited for his eyes to stop watering. When his vision cleared, a man stood before him. The man whistled confidently with his hands in the pockets of a fashionable khaki suit, topped with a matching hat decorated with a duck feather. The man smiled at Bruno with only his upper lip.

"At last, Bruno." The stranger leaned forward and patted Bruno on the head.

Bruno looked back suspiciously. The stranger spoke Bruno's language in an accent he couldn't recognize. His self-assured posture was unsettling, and his familiarity even more so.

"Oh you don't have to worry. Your mother made all the arrangements before she..." the man paused dramatically and looked at his dazzling polished shoes. "...passed from this world."

After spending half a year with some truly low individuals, Bruno had learned how to spot a confidence man from a mile away. The stranger was one of them.

"You can trust me, Bruno," he smiled, flashing innumerable large teeth.

"Then tell me my mother's name," Bruno commanded, in a voice comically serious for such a young man.

"Djuna Schulz," the stranger responded happily. He followed this with a forced frown and said, "May God rest her soul."

The stranger leaned forward.

"I know an excellent restaurant a few blocks from here. Come, young Bruno. It's all been arranged."

Slowly, Bruno rose to his feet. The stranger held a hand to help steady him, but Bruno refused. He picked up his box, saddled it under his arm, and stood facing the stranger.

"Tell me your name," Bruno commanded.

"You'll simply love this restaurant, young Bruno. It's like nothing you've seen before. I hope you brought your appetite," the man laughed. He set out ahead of Bruno and zigzagged down the sidewalk, nearly out of sight. Bruno scurried after him, slow to keep up, struggling under the weight of his box.

*   *   *

Indeed, Bruno had never seen such a spread before. He ate until he felt the food packing up to the top of his throat, and then ate more. All the while the stranger picked on a single beef rib, eating slowly and methodically, cleaning it like a coyote. Few words were spoken between them, and any question Bruno asked was ignored or dodged by the man.

Outside the restaurant, Bruno was sluggish and exhausted from the feast.

"Thank you," Bruno croaked.

The stranger turned to Bruno, his face set in an unnerving grin. His cheekbones were high, smiling without his eyes.

"Of course, young Bruno. I have more to show you still!" Again the stranger leapt away from Bruno. They weaved around hurrying businessmen. Bruno couldn't help but bump into them, for his eyes were fixed on the towering buildings above.

They were a few blocks away from the restaurant when Bruno stopped dead.

"My box!" Bruno yelped. He turned around to head back and the stranger didn't follow.

"Come, I need it!" he shouted. The stranger didn't move. He shouted again to no response.

"Curse you!" Bruno yelled at the stranger. At this, the stranger laughed like a madman. Bruno huffed and went the other way down the street.

However this street was not the street he had been on just moments ago. The buildings were smaller, two stories tall at most. No one walked the sidewalks and the streets were much narrower. He could hear the clopping of a horse in the distance but could not see it.

Scared, Bruno turned back to find the stranger, and that street had also changed. What moments before looked like the throbbing heart of a cosmopolis was now sparse. In the distance, the cobblestone road turned into dirt, wandering off into a country road on the horizon. The sun began retreating under the shingled roofs of the lonely storefronts.

Not a single candle burned in the windows, save for a single house. Bruno approached it. Above the door was wood lettering that spelled "RESTAURANT" in Bruno's language. Desperate for help, he opened the massive door. It screeched on its hinges like it was wheezing in pain.

The hallway was completely dark and smelled like rotting newspaper.

"Hello!" Bruno shouted into the darkness. His voice was muffled, as if he were surrounded on all sides by heavy curtains. Thrown into panic, he turned around to feel for the door and found nothing. He moved forward with his hands out and his heart racing.

Staggering in the dark, Bruno took a step but his foot found no floor. He hurtled forward and fell down an invisible staircase. His elbow cracked on a stair, and he screamed, only to be cut short by falling to a stop, face-first on cold ground.

The pain danced over him while he collected himself. When he opened his eyes, he saw a sliver of light coming from a crack between curtains. He limped through them and entered a dimly lit red room with velvet walls and empty tables with candles burning. On one of the tables sat his box.

Bruno wobbled to the table to collect it. He sat and rested his head on the polished oak when he felt a hand on his shoulder.

It was the stranger. Bruno gasped. The stranger stared through him with jet black eyes and smiled. His mouth was filled with hundreds of sharp teeth, row after row disappearing into the back of his mouth.

"The dance," the stranger hissed.

The lights went out. Through the curtains ambled out a

big brown bear in a vest wearing a fez. The trained bear sat on a stool and spun the arm of a sound box. It squeaked with a rusty whine and made a chilling plucking noise, like a broken piano.

The curtains behind the bear waved, and out came a woman in a burlesque dress. She swayed from side to side, her face white like a doll and eyes vacant. Bruno froze with boiling fear.

It was his mother.

The stranger clapped and danced, hooting and spinning to the deathly tune of the bear's sound box. Bruno tried to scream but could not.

His mother approached his table and pulled herself up, dancing and kicking. Bruno grabbed onto the bottom of her dress and screamed.

"Mama! Mama!" he shouted. She didn't look down neither did she stop dancing.

"Mama! Mama listen to me!" he shouted, pleading with the automaton.

She danced and danced as the stranger spun in circles around Bruno. Bruno's box began to smolder on the table, quickly igniting in flames. It burned with tongues of fire shooting to the ceiling but did not consume the table nor the room.

"Dance, dance!" the stranger commanded. Bruno didn't move.

"Dance," his mother croaked, staring at nothing. Bruno wept.

The Stranger grabbed Bruno by the armpits and set him on the table. He wrapped Bruno's arms around his mother's waist. Her dress was freezing and soaking wet. He tried to pull his hands free, but they were stuck to a noxious slime that coated her.

"Dance!" the stranger screamed. He whirled in circles,

clapping as the bear played the sound box hypnotically.

Bruno wept insanely, holding onto his mother. She twirled and kicked and danced as he slid to her feet.

The stranger spun in circles like a demented ballerina. Bruno's mother kicked and held up her skirt. He collapsed on the table, screaming and begging for it to end.

Bruno felt fingers dig into his collarbone. He yelped and snapped his head back. There was the stranger, sneering at him with implacable menace.

"DANCE!" he commanded, his infinite rows of teeth glistening in his mouth.

"DANCE! DANCE! DANCE!"

Bruno raised his feet and swayed with his mother while the stranger cackled. His hands began to freeze on his mother's hips and he could not let go. They turned purple with cold and his fingernails turned black.

The stranger clapped wildly, knocking over chairs and screaming like a madman as Bruno danced.

The dance would last forever.

The Story Must Be Told

Seasons of the Story

AFTER THE ATTACK

The 77th Story ⇡

Thousands of soggy Rice Krispies coagulate and form a solid, amorphous ball in the bowl of lukewarm milk in front of me. Through the walls an ambulance siren fades into silence. The cupboards sparkle from Clorox and the fridge is a menagerie of drawings in crayon and fat markers. The last remnants of glitter unstick from construction paper in hanging strips of Elmer's glue.

These are Ben's drawings. A visual timeline of when he started scribbling at age two, to eight months and twelve days into Kindergarten.

Across the table is Ben's seat. There too a glob of Rice Krispies sinks into gray milk. His spoon is set perfectly next to the bowl, resting on a paper napkin printed with pictures of Spongebob Squarepants, Patrick and Squidward. Squidward's fists are clenched in anger, his brow furrowed and eyeballs bloodshot.

⇡ By: P. Lane Crash. From: The Songs of Greasy Greg.

13

I look at my own Spongebob napkin. The ink bleeds watercolor circles beneath my damp spoon. I lift one scoop of cereal, hover it over the five-day-old stubble of my chin, suspend it back over the bowl and pour it back in. I think the last time I ate was lunch yesterday, but I can't remember.

Ben is not in his seat.

My mouth is thick and dry. I can smell my bad breath. A hangover orbits around the inside of my skull, sawing it from the inside out in a low electric hum of pain.

Leslie walks into the kitchen wearing an earthy orange blouse tucked into autumn-appropriate forest green velvet pants. She stomps to the back door and holds herself against the wall with her right arm, her bare feet fishing for her shoes in a longer line of shoes pushed up against the baseboard: Ben's L.A. Gear light-up sneakers, dress shoes for grandma's and yellow rubber rain boots that match the rain jacket hanging on the coatrack by the front door. Leslie faces away, neither does she acknowledge me.

My temper simmers. I grind my teeth.

Her slumped shoulders reveal she didn't sleep last night. It hurts to bend my neck. I woke up at 3 a.m. from a blackout with my hands asleep, folded on my chest. My knees were sore from resting over the arm of the couch. The ceiling fan spun slowly, its blades covered in a layer of dust and drywall, scented with the smoke we couldn't wash out of the walls. I had a murky buzz and already had a headache. I dreaded waking up as I flipped off the lights, turned off the TV, and laid back down on my side to sleep.

Leslie is looking for her Metrocard so she can walk four miles to the only operating subway in Brooklyn, loop into lower Manhattan, wait at least an hour to board one of *two* working trains in Manhattan, and linger outside Ben's old school to look for Ben who will not be there.

"If I were a five-year-old boy, the last place on Earth you'd find me is school," I say, my words slow and voice deep, quivering with exhausted anger.

"Ben likes school," she says without looking up, digging through her purse.

I swallow and blink hard.

"If he shows up at school, they'll call us," I say even slower.

"I don't trust them."

"Of course you don't."

"I trust myself."

"Not me?"

"No," she says emotionlessly. She unzips the small pocket in her purse and pulls out her Metrocard. She faces me.

"Leslie—"

She cuts me off.

"You can stay here today. Today could be the day."

"Today won't be the day and I promise you—I promise—the day isn't coming."

For an instant, Leslie's eyes wince at my words. They quickly go blank again.

"Have a good day," she says. It sounds like a threat.

I say nothing as she opens the door, goes out, and carefully closes it behind her. If she slammed the door, I would have gotten the last word. But the last word is hers. She's won another argument with the unbeatable weapon of emotionless self-control.

I leave our cereal bowls where they are and go to the bathroom to brush my teeth. When I spit out the foamy toothpaste it's lightly tinted pink. I lean close to the mirror, careful not to look at my face, and lift up my upper lip to inspect my gums. The faintest trace of blood clings to my molars at the gumline. I rinse with

Listerine and it stings even after I spit.

Back in the kitchen, I jam my foot into my shoes and the heel folds. I bend my leg up and dig it out, and the shoe slips on. I put on my jacket and sling my messenger bag over my shoulder. I go out the front door and down the steps and into the street to join the small packs of people walking from Brooklyn to work in Manhattan.

Cars rot on flat, waterlogged tires on the sides of the road, immobilized from the thousands of electromagnetic pulses. Across the street, a crater still smolders behind a hastily-made lead barricade. It smokes even after these two years from the plasma blast that obliterated the block across the way but left ours untouched. I suspect my gums are bleeding from radiation emitted by the impact site. The government says we have nothing to worry about. I'm not worried. I don't care.

The National Guard has checkpoints set up every twenty blocks. Bored soldiers joke with one another, their sterilizing alpha radiation rifles slung over their shoulders, pointed at the asphalt with the safety on. The soldiers' casual attitude doesn't suggest we'll be prepared if it comes back.

Helicopters *plut plut plut* over deserted neighborhoods and unseen jets roar and split the heavy clouds above us with sonic booms. I still flinch every time they break the sound barrier.

On the horizon, the Manhattan skyline is a shattered skeleton of skyscrapers. It looks like blackened, broken teeth. Smoke still pours from the long-evacuated southern tip of the city and midtown is almost entirely missing. It looks like a perfect rectangle has been excised from the island.

It's 7:54 a.m. and I should arrive to work on time.

* * *

It's 11:17 a.m. I'm trying not to doze off in the drop-ceiling conference room of Clubhouse Marketing and Media.

Evan, a twenty-something turd from Los Angeles, pitches us a new campaign for Golden Bear Brewery. Their flagship beer is called No Bullshit Porter. On the label a muscular, bearded cartoon man presses his work boot on a dead bear's throat, one of his hairy arms held in the air in victory. This is Clubhouse Marketing and Media's wheelhouse. We manufacture and sell manliness. I would do something else but I wouldn't know what to do.

Evan came with hordes of other young opportunists looking for an easy-in to a decimated job market, oversaturated with federal money to keep people from leaving New York City. A disaster prospector.

He gives us a shitty, overconfident grin and raises his eyebrows up and down like a bad actor. He dramatically takes a breath.

"What do you think when you hear *New York City?* What do you see in your mind?"

I see Ben at three years old, asleep in his stroller. Leslie pushes him through the Brooklyn Botanic Garden. It's sunny and the air is clear. There are no helicopters and no soldiers. No metallic crunching of tank treads. The perimeter is lined with an ornate iron fence instead of caution tape printed with biohazard symbols.

I look around the table. Eight of my eleven colleagues were in New York when it happened. Duncan's scarred face goes white and his ears turn red. He stares at the table and takes a drink of water without looking up. It spills down his tie.

Julie breathes quickly. She twists her bracelet, squeezing her late husband's birthstone between her fingers. Her eyes sear straight through the imbecile at the front of the room who doesn't notice.

Gene sighs and slouches forward, resting his cheek on his balled fist.

Gene was not in New York at the time. Gene's son Chris certainly was. Chris who was my best friend. Gene walked all the way from Hudson-on-Croton to the Triboro Bridge, only to be turned around under threat of arrest by a Marine as strange technicolor explosions ripped apart Manhattan and Chris along with it.

A few months after the event, after we all went back to work, Gene accidentally called me Chris. He pretended it didn't happen and I did too. He called out sick the next day and was out for the following month. He came back to work looking tired and has looked tired ever since.

Gene clears his throat to speak and Evan cuts him off.

"No no, don't answer yet. I guarantee the TV can answer for us." Evan winks and picks up the remote for the too-wide television behind him. He clicks it on.

A Jeep Grand Cherokee plows through the desert, a red cloud of dust trailing it. There's a Jeep Sales Event in New Jersey. The commercial fades into another. An American flag waves.

"Jesus Christ," I mutter to myself loud enough for everyone to hear.

The American flag gives way to George Clooney's deep voice over scenes from that day.

"A city was asked to stand up," he narrates. A drone captures a beautiful, chilling shot of the old Manhattan. There's a still frame of a soldier pulling her wounded comrade away from a crater. Behind them, a building is collapsing, engulfed in an orb of blue plasma.

"Our nation came together. Coca-Cola led the charge—"

"Turn this off, you little prick," I bark. Evan rolls his eyes with his shitty smirk and turns off the TV. Across the desk, Duncan sadly smiles at me.

"Wrap it up, Evan," Gene exhales.

"New Yorkers are tough. New Yorkers are heroes," he leads.

That word again.

"New Yorkers deserve a beer that is more than a label. A beer that reflects who they are. That's why I want to show you..." he pauses and clicks on the projector on the side of the room. Two sweating beer bottles shine on the wall.

"Liberty Lager and Hero's Tears. Golden Bear wants to penetrate the Northeast Market with a Weissbeer. I think Hero's Tears is the way to do it."

His fucking smirk.

Liberty Lager's label portrays a busty Statue of Liberty with red lipstick. The real Statue of Liberty melted into a solid disk of copper and lives on the bottom of the Hudson River a half mile away. Hero's Tears features a serious firefighter.

I stand abruptly, knocking my chair against the wall.

"Gotta admit it hits a nerve, eh, Peter?" he condescends.

Thirty-two blocks away, Leslie tries to blend in across from Ben's school, desperately searching for him. Careful not to be seen by the school administration and warned they'll call the police if they see her again, even though they'd never make the call.

I'm lifting Evan up by his collar and I slam him against the drywall. The TV rattles with every shove. His cowardly eyes go wide and helpless.

"Let him go, Peter," Gene says without urgency. My

colleagues look on in a mix of shock and satisfaction.

Gene stands up. He addresses us, neither does he separate the frakas.

"That's fine, Evan. Pitch it to Golden Bear and keep me in the loop. C'mon Peter," he says. I give Evan one more look that assures him I'd kill him if only I could, and I let him back down. He gathers himself as I back away, my eyes fixed on his shitty face.

"Pff, fucking drunk psycho," he mutters. I lunge forward, palm his face, and bounce his head off the wall. He crumbles to the floor, holding his temples.

"I'll fucking sue your ass," he threatens.

"You won't," I tell him. I leave the room. No one helps him up as he brings himself to his feet.

Gene waits at the door and motions for me to follow him out.

"The campaign is shit but it'll make money," he says absently.

"I d'know, Gene," I say.

"Don't worry."

Gene stops.

"Hey. Peter."

"Mm?"

He clears his throat. He starts to speak but stops. His blue eyes have a sheen of implacable sadness and his skin is gray. He looks like he's shrunk since yesterday.

"I'm just tired is all," he says strangely, as if answering a question. He clasps my shoulder but doesn't look me in the face. Without another word, he goes into his office and shuts the door. I lean against the wall as adrenaline tapers out of my bloodstream.

I look at my hands. They're shaking.

At home in our upstairs hallway, there are five framed

pictures. Each year we dipped Ben's right hand in green paint and pressed it against a sheet of paper. Ben Age 1 to Ben Age 5 progresses down the hall, his hand growing.

A gunshot blasts in Gene's office and splits the air. My ears ring and adrenaline returns in force. I open the door and Gene is slumped over, the side of his face resting on his desk. His right eye is pink with blood and the other stares at me. Blood pours from his mouth, nose and ears, and the back of his head has a massive hole. It looks like someone lamely tossed a shovel of brains on the wall behind and floor below to him. He loosely holds a handgun. I swallow. It smells like gunpowder and iron.

"Call an ambulance," I mutter behind me.

I walk into Gene's office and approach his body. I put my hand on his back. I kneel and open his bottom right-hand drawer. In it is an unopened, twenty-five year bottle of Johnnie Walker Blue that Chris got Gene for his sixtieth birthday. I open it and take a pull.

I softly knock it twice against Gene's shoulder, offering him a drink.

I don't know why.

I head out to the exit without grabbing my coat or bag. Bored and tired paramedics pass me on the stairs without urgency. I wonder how many suicides they've seen.

I exit the building. There are no cars in the streets, only pedestrians. Helicopters chop above.

The Metlife building has a perfect circle cut in it from a solid pulse of plasma that blasted through it those years ago. It's been preserved and apparently will be a monument. "MET" has blown off, leaving only "LIFE" in big block letters. Many refuse to believe this is a coincidence.

I take a long pull of scotch then vomit on the sidewalk.

* * *

The meeting with Weissman and Schulz ended early and on a high note. Chris and I pitched them, "The Future Is Yours. Let Us Worry About It." Seemingly contradictory, but they bought it. We chatted in the atrium of the building for a second and I declined an early happy hour. It was only 3 p.m. and I planned to surprise Ben and pick him up from school. No clouds. Warm in the sun and chilly in the shade. We'd take the bridge.

I gave Chris a hug goodbye. The next time I'd see his face would be on a half-covered missing person poster in Union Square.

I hid behind a Ford Taurus and waited for Ben. If a teacher or crossing guard saw me, they'd mistake me for a pervert. But I was stealthy. Ben walked out alone between small groups of friends and I jumped out to scare him. His face lit up and I scooped him up. I asked if he wanted to walk over the bridge and he nodded.

He excitedly told me a circuitous, confusing story about his school day and I was happy to hear it. He held my first two fingers in his tiny hand as Avenue A became Essex and we turned on Delancey towards the Williamsburg Bridge.

Confused, terrified tourists on Citi Bikes weaved into the pedestrian lanes as we climbed up the bridge. Ben asked if we could have pizza and I couldn't see why not.

I took out my phone to text Leslie when a sonic boom cracked through the air, rattling the bridge. The struts gave a rusty iron wheeze as the supports gently swung. Instinctively, I jumped on top of Ben and held him to the ground. He screamed.

A fighter jet must have gone right above us. A passenger plane must have slammed into another and crashed into midtown. Jesus Christ, there must have been a bomb. Dirty? Improvised?

Nuclear? Then I turned and saw it.

A sickly blue, electric portal shaped like a cat's eye opened over Manhattan. A gigantic, half-mile wide monster coiled out of it. The monster's giant head opened like a mouse trap and spat a single stream of blue plasma towards the financial district. The buildings burned in an odd way, as if covered in electric napalm. They started on fire but didn't smoke, rather disintegrated into the ground. The monster wound out of its interstellar portal and was nearly the length of Manhattan. It slithered through the air like a water snake, smashing the tops of buildings under its belly, sending debris onto the streets below.

People stampeded toward Brooklyn. I ran the mile without stopping, holding Ben tight against me with my hand on the back of his head. I told him to keep his eyes shut so he wouldn't see the destruction behind him. He cried quietly but was otherwise silent.

People were trampled. People leapt from the bridge.

We were nearly down the ramp when Ben broke into a blood curdling scream. Others screamed and the crowd moved faster.

I turned and saw the monster appear over the bridge. It had a massive, terrible mouth, nor did it have eyes. The monster reeled back and vomited a ray of plasma at us. The blue streak hit the tower on the Brooklyn-side of the bridge. The bridge fell back, the cables snapping, flying back into the air towards the monster. The wayward cables sliced open the monster's exoskeleton and orange fluid leaked out. The monster turned back to the island.

The cables snapped back towards us, splitting the middle of the bridge longways. It caved.

I don't know how Ben slipped from my arms, but Ben slipped from my arms. I heard him scream once and saw his hand reaching out for me between terrified, stampeding people. He went down. I saw his hand fall to the concrete. I saw a shoe then a boot then more feet trample it as the current of people carried me down the ramp and onto Barry street.

I couldn't get back to him. It was impossible. There was no gap in the herd. There was no way. There was nothing I could do.

People poured out. Bloodied. Horrified.

I couldn't save him.

* * *

Leslie lays on her side, asleep in her clothes. My mouth is dry and sour from liquor and vomit and liquor. It's 2:12 a.m. One of her heels is on the floor and the other hangs from her toes, her leg protruding off the bed. Ben's Paw Patrol cup is in my hand but the thought of water nauseates me.

I sit on the end of the bed and Leslie grunts softly.

I stare at my hands. I look at my index finger and my middle finger. I can feel Ben's fist wrapped around them. I can hear his voice.

I take a sip of water and my temples throb.

"I was with Ben," I tell Leslie. "I surprised him at school. We went over the bridge."

Aside from Leslie's breathing, it is silent.

"I don't know why I didn't tell you. I didn't not tell you to protect you, either. It was me. I didn't want to hear myself say it. It was too much. What I saw. I didn't care if you knew or not. I didn't want to know."

I sip.

"I saw Ben die. It wasn't the monster. Well, it was. But he was trampled. I saw him go down. I couldn't get back."

Leslie groans and takes a breath. She doesn't turn. She speaks softly.

"I know, Peter."

I don't cry and I can't swallow.

"You talk in your sleep," she whispers.

I sit in silence. I don't feel any less guilty. No weight lifts from my shoulders.

"Will you come with me tomorrow? We can wait for Ben."

I clench my two first fingers with my other fist. I squeeze and imagine it's Ben.

"Of course," I tell Leslie. "Of course we can."

Her breathing slows to the rhythm of sleep.

I want to touch her but I can't.

I get up and go downstairs. I turn on the TV and flip on the lights. I lay on my back and watch the ceiling fan spin.

George Clooney's voice comes from the speakers. "Our nation came together. Coca-Cola led the charge."

The Story Must Be Told

THE BOYS OPEN

The 37th Story ⇡

The wife and I had been saving pennies for two years to afford the tickets. The day we reached the sum we needed, we both cried, holding each other—we had worked and scrimped so hard, eating half portions for weeks of rumbling guts and food-starved dreams. The day the tickets went on sale, I arrived five hours early, only to find a line of more experienced buyers stretching around the block, all of them having slept the night before on the pavement by the Onsetters Building. I counted them all best I could, wrangled the arithmetic in my head, and rightfully feared I would not be able to purchase tickets. I was wrong.

Six hours in the baking sun later, I was the last of the common people to purchase a ticket, and I ran home promptly after, my hand clutched to my breast pocket as though racing a heart attack. I threw the door open to our woefully modest home, and saw the wife with a hoop of cross stitch half-heartedly

---

⇡ By: Sweetcorn Hotcorn.

threaded on her lap. She didn't even have to ask, having seen my expression, and we joined arms and leaped and laughed with the tears on our cheeks. Our prayers were answered:

We would attend the Boys Open.

Four days. Three thousand boys! Competitions of strength, dexterity, fashion, and breeding. The Boys Open came to our province every six years, tickets seized by the white wigs in the local government, and the barons and baronesses in their boutique formal wear. But this year the Lord had favored me to witness the boys of all the empire's nations with my own eyes.

The week preceding the opening events were a blur of dream—I found it hard to believe my feet walked solid ground, convinced I was floating. The wife had continued to starve herself, saving her own stipend for lip creams and eye chalk, making room for extra tugs of corset lace so that she could shine among the noblewomen of the festivities.

When the first day arrived, we skipped the trolley and walked the whole way in our finest dress, giving neighbors a peek of our hard-earned privilege.

"Say hullo to the boys!" the grocer laughed.

"The boys! The boys!" the children squealed in their orbits about us, two shining stars.

"Harumph!" the milk maiden scoffed, churning her butter with spite.

The jealousy, the adoration, it was as though the wife and I were boys ourselves.

Though only a scant portion of seats—the least favorable of vantages, mind you—were open to commoners, the mob before the common entrance was violent. Scalpers and thieves practiced their craft upon the dim-witted and distracted, fathers fought to control their children, mothers sought to rein in their husbands, and horses, not understanding the commotion, shat on the dirt.

    The wife and I pressed ourselves into the throng, inching closer to the gates. A woman in front of us was denied entrance—her tickets were forgeries, expensive ones, too. She had to be escorted away by guards, such was her fury, her shattered expectation. The moment before the agent approved our tickets, my brow spurted quarts of perspiration, sure at the crucial moment we would be denied. The wife's hand gripped mine until it felt needles.

    "Enjoy the boys," the agent winked.

    We were in.

    The Open began with the Parade of Boys. Though we were too high in the stands to make out facial features, the sheer variety of boys was enough to steal our breath. The wife gathered a scorecard from a nearby vendor, and we marked each type of boy we saw. First came the small boys, then the medium boys, then the rotund husky boys, whose waists even I envied. Boys of brown pigment, soft tan, white, and pink, with shining black hair and clean shaven heads, boys whose hair hid their necks and upper backs like girls—but were boys all the same.

    Despite the excitement, the wife put into words a weight that was tugging at my heart.

    "Such a waste," she sighed. I squeezed her palm.

    A gap formed in the line of parading boys, and the final boy was carried out. He was the winning boy from the Open six years prior, and as was tradition, he was carried out upon a skeletal throne built from the debris of defeated boys. He was now only thirteen years old, I would guess. He must have been a fierce competitor to defeat so many boys at only seven years of age the last Open. In old times, he may have grown to be a general, a president, but those were days of barbarians, democracies. It was better this way.

    The next three days showcased the best the empire's boys could offer. They leapt, they swam, they fought, and they gave their bodies to measurement with calipers and scales. The wife and I instantly agreed on our favorite to win, a boy with a muscular build and strong knees, who had decimated the competition in the deadlift. He was modest, which we admired, and as the next competition showcased, he could spit farther than any man I had seen, and woman I had loved. A boy for the ages, the wife and I agreed.

    His next win during the formal wear competition was such a surprising triumph that half the stadium was on its feet, chanting in full-throated unison: "One True Boy. One True Boy." When he was bested at the tight rope walk on the third day, it was hard not to take the defeat personally. We were not alone in the loss, for when they lowered his bound, squirming body to the meat thrashers, our cries mingled with others. *Could we not save one boy?* Surely he could replace a mule in the field, a stallion in the breeding pits. I saw wealthier patrons, for whom the Boys Open was a minor distraction, gather their servants and leave after his destruction—a show of gaudy protest. The wife and I would have joined them were this not a singular event in our lives. We did not anticipate our champion would take the crown—no—but if nothing else, we could get our money's worth.

    On the final day of festivities, only fifteen boys remained, including the wry thirteen-year-old carried in on the pyre of skeletons. The ultimate competition left strength and agility behind, and tested the boys on the most critical of traits: endurance.

    Each boy climbed a wooden pillar without aid, and stood

atop the narrow circular ledge, toes gripping the edges. A band of lutes and accordions played the empire's anthem three times through, as agents of the Boys Open stacked tinder, kindling, and great logs of fuel beneath each pillar. On the final note of groaning accordion, the gamesmaster twirled the traditional green and purple patterned flag, and the fires were started. Two boys lost their balance immediately, one coughing from smoke inhalation, and they fell twenty feet to the ground with a crunch of shattered bone. Agents met their skulls with clubs and maces so as not to distract the remaining competitors with their cries. The crowd alternated between roars and hushed reverence, enthralled by every wobble of form, every cough of lungs, every stifled cry of burned flesh.

    The thirteen remaining boys stood equal for five minutes before the flames took their toll. In a flash, two wooden pillars were striped with flame, climbing until the boys at top, steadfast in their position, were consumed in fire. The crowd gave a polite clap—this was the honorable way to lose.

    Twenty more minutes passed, and nine other boys were taken out of contest. Three fell, five were consumed, and one pillar collapsed having been weakened by flame—luck was just as much reason to lose—and the agents promptly clubbed the unfortunate boy's skull. Impressively, the last winner was still among the two standing, and as the other competitor's pillar streaked with orange, and his feet began to smoke, it was clear he would win again—or so we thought.

    The former winner, seeing how close he was to the end, broke his forward gaze. He peered to the ground, with all the concern of having dropped a coin.

    Then he jumped.

    A gasp arose instantaneously from the thousands

watching, and the boy whose feet blistered and charred could hardly believe the sight. While agents clubbed the old winner's brain, others extinguished the new winner's flames. He was a ten-year-old boy from the Eastern Province, with a shiny mat of black hair and healthy bronze skin.

The wife and I stayed in our seats as the rest of the crowd left for the attached banquet halls. We took stock of the landscape—there was where an island boy held his breath for three whole minutes. Over there was where a rare red-headed boy was impaled by spikes. There was where our One True Boy fell from the tightrope and earned his fate with the other losers. It was the greatest contest of sport we had ever seen.

Minutes later, we were in the banquet room, where the meat of the boys was gathered in delicate trays for the rich, covered in gravy on troughs for us common. By the time we took our plates to the front of the line, it was mostly face parts and fingers left, but there was meat enough to salvage.

We laughed, playing with our food, poking each other with the fingers and trying on new ears for size. Nearby nobles turned their noses at our play.

"Have they no respect for the games?" they asked, stuffing rib meat into their swollen cheeks.

We paid no mind. Like all but one of the boys, this would most likely be our only Boys Open.

Riding the trolley home that night, the wife asked me if we could somehow attend it again in six years. I put a hand to my neck.

"It's hard to say. I was fortunate to earn the salary I have this year, and if we wish to buy a plot then we shouldn't really—"

The wife sighed and laid her head on my shoulder, rocking

gently in the half-full trolley. I hated to disappoint her like that.

"Unless, of course, we have a boy of our own one day." She smiled up to me.

"Do you mean it?"

"I don't see why not. Any boy can enter the qualifying rounds. And even parents of boys cut in initial rounds have preference for buying tickets."

"He'd have to be born soon."

"Then we'll start tonight," I said with a kiss, then slowly, a slip of tongue.

How hopeful we were, how we glowed! Truly, it was hard not to find the spirit lifted, the heart strengthened, and vows reaffirmed after such majesty as our first Boys Open.

The Story Must Be Told

DICK DVORAK BOWLS A PERFECT GAME

The 94th Story ⇧

CHAPTER 1: DICK DVORAK, HERO

It was Dick Dvorak's fourth night on the late shift at Armonde's Cool Air and Refrigeration. His eyes were heavy and his hands clumsy as he typed updated schematics into the QuikPunch 1000. He entered code to reprogram the machine, slowing down the puncher springs by a few milliseconds, and dialed back the revolutions of the production rollers.

Dick was a wiz with gadgets. He could do anything from making a clock radio out of spare circuit boards, to programming a $300,000 piece of industrial machinery. He wore a digital watch that he'd made himself—a source of great pride.

Dick ran the new sequence and fired up the QuikPunch 1000. It began pounding innumerable divots into steel fan guards

---

⇧ By: Too Sweet, Glop Glop, Sniff Sniff the Elder.

on industrial HVAC units. The endless *pu-thunk, pu-thunk, pu-thunk* of the pneumatic hammer lulled him into a mixed state of hypnosis and exhaustion.

He was in a bad mood and was not looking forward to the end of his shift. Dick and the late shift always went bowling Tuesday mornings once they clocked out. He was on the hook to go. All he could think about was his bed.

Dick was nodding off when a high-pitched, earsplitting scream from the freon seal station broke him out of his trance. He hit the stop button on the QuickPunch 1000 and swung around to see Patty O'Reardon staggering backward as a white cloud of gas blasted him in the face.

Freon erupted from a crack in the pipe. A fracture split up to the connecting pipe above. The nut that held them together began to vibrate itself out of place, and in moments it would be weaponized under the pressure.

Dick sprinted to Patty and tackled him to the ground right as the pipe burst, shooting twisted metal inches above Patty's head before it exploded against the wall behind them. Dick felt a tiny, sharp sensation on his forehead, like he'd been lightly scraped by a burning cat claw. The pain did not last.

Dave Janek, the senior assembly manager, pulled the emergency shut-off lever. The freon leak slowed, and the remaining gas trickled out of the burst pipe like steam rising off coffee.

Dick rose to his knees and slapped Patty on the face to keep him awake. Patty's skin was blistering, and his eyelids were cracked and bleeding. A mixture of tears and blood ran down his face from his burned-out eyes.

"C'mon buddy," Dick whispered to Patty. "We gotta get you washed off. Call an ambulance!" Dick shouted over his shoulder. He pulled Patty to his feet, grunting as he led him to the chemical shower. Dick yanked the cord and acrid blue liquid sprayed them.

"It's okay, buddy," Dick assured him. Patty whimpered as Dick bent him over the eye wash station and tended Patty's wounds. Watching a nearly 300-pound man cry made Dick feel ill and his forehead began to throb. The room was spinning as the paramedics arrived and led Patty away.

Dick panted, his clothes soaked in the blue fluid. It dripped down his bald head, over the cut on his forehead, and clung to his shirt, already tight over his generous beer belly. He wiped off his eyes and saw the night shift gathered before him in a semicircle. They began to clap, slowly reaching a crescendo. Some were tearing up. Others pumped their fists into the air.

Dave Janek approached Dick and put his arm around him.

"That's one hell of a brave thing you did, Dick." Dave looked at him and paused. "You're a hero."

Dick let the word wash over him. "Hero."

He did feel like a hero.

"You got a little cut there. Looks like it's bruising. Want me to call the medics back?"

"Yeah, if you pay for the ambulance," Dick smirked. The night shift cracked up.

"I'll drive you home as soon as you wash this shit off you," Dave laughed, patting Dick on the back. Adrenaline pulsed through Dick's veins. He was a hero.

Dick took a deep breath. "I thought we were going bowling."

Dave smiled and grabbed Dick's hand, raising it above them in triumph. "We're going bowling!" he shouted.

The night shift erupted in applause and laughter as a tiny, nearly invisible drop of blood eeked out of Dick's wound, drying immediately.

Two inches behind the wound, behind a medically inappreciable fracture in his skull, a 1-millimeter long and razor-thin piece of stainless steel pipe was lodged in his prefrontal cortex. His brain slowly bled as he headed for the showers.

CHAPTER 2: A TRAGEDY, A PERFECT GAME

Lynne Browne rolled the ball down the lane but failed to pick up the spare. She crooked her head with a frustrated smirk as she watched the clunking steel arm swipe away the ten pin into the bowels of its machinery.

"Still warming up," she said to no one as she returned to her seat. "You're up, hero." She winked at Dick.

TVs hung from the ceiling above them, playing endless loops of SportsCenter.

Dick went to the ball return, rubbing his faintly throbbing forehead. He held his hand over the small grate to dry his palm.

He checked his handmade watch and saw the time turn from 8:47 a.m. to 8:48 a.m. The digital display reminded him it was Tuesday. After all the excitement, it felt like a Friday.

Dick scooped up his ball and headed for the foul line. He held it in front of his face and squared his legs. He took a deep breath, pictured himself hitting a strike, swung his arm, and sent the ball down the approach. It wavered by the gutter, nearly dropping in, when the spin took over and it careened into the one pin. The pin deck exploded in a strike.

Dick clenched his hand in a fist and pumped his arm.

"Woo-wee!" Dave Janek cried behind him. His team was on their feet, clapping. Lynne gave him two thumbs up. Ernie Powell folded his thick arms and nodded with a smile.

"You're the man, Mr. Hero!" Ernie shouted. Dick returned a thumbs up and smiled.

Dick maintained his concentration like a yogi. He ritualized his throw: Approach the ball return. Dry hand. Check watch. Envision the strike. Hit the strike.

By the ninth frame, a small crowd had gathered around him as he hit the one pin for yet another strike. The bowling alley went wild.

He sat in his chair, closed his eyes, and breathed slowly. He took himself far away from the bowling alley, clearing his head entirely, seeing only a white slate in his mind's eye. He whispered, "Hero," his new mantra.

Dick went up for his final turn. Three strikes away from a perfect game. He picked up the first strike without hesitating. The alley erupted in cheers as he picked up his ball from the return.

He began his ritual and threw the ball when his right foot slipped ever so slightly, giving the ball a weird spin. It slowly zigzagged, inches away from dropping into the gutter, when it suddenly turned, hit the one and two pins simultaneously, and delivered Dick another strike.

He stayed where he was and took a deep breath, resting his hands on his hips. He replayed his mistake in his mind, envisioned himself rolling again with a corrected stance, and watched himself get another strike.

He opened his eyes as the ball returned. He sunk his fingers into the holes and rolled for the last time. He watched it easily slide down the approach, his concentration broken for only a second when he heard an electronic click from the TVs changing channels behind him.

A woman screamed, "Oh my GOD!" right as he landed the final strike.

Dick spun around, his hands in the air. Tears streamed down his face. He cried out in ecstasy and fell to his knees.

The alley was silent. Everyone was staring at the TVs, their faces paralyzed in shock and horror. He joined the crowd and looked up.

All twenty screens were set to CNN, each showing smoke pouring out of the World Trade Center's North Tower.

The footage cut to a toothy news anchor. His face was sickly white, set beneath carefully styled hair. He spoke.

"At 8:48 this morning, a commercial airplane struck the World Trade Center. Initial reports indicate…"

Dick felt dizzy as the reporter droned on. Defeated, he dropped into his seat and rubbed his throbbing forehead.

His perfect moment had been ripped away from him.

It wasn't fair.

He had bowled the perfect game.

CHAPTER 3: A HERO UNREMEMBERED

That night on the late shift, Dick's heroic rescue of Patty O'Reardon was all but forgotten, nor did anyone mention his perfect game. He waited in vain all evening for someone to mention either, along with a pat on the back or a casual muttering of "hero."

In the break room, Dick's co-workers had their eyes fixed to the TV. Burning papers snowed down on Manhattan. The rubble looked like the epicenter of a nuclear attack. The news began calling the fiery pit "Ground Zero."

Dick sighed. His head hurt. He knew he should be feeling sad but he felt angry and cast aside by his co-workers.

Dave Janek entered the room, vacantly holding a cup of coffee he did not sip. Dick quickly went over to him.

"How's, uh, Patty doing, after my heroic rescue?" he asked, barely concealing a smirk.

"Patty?" Dave was confused. "Patty, my wife, Patty?"

"O'Reardon!" Dick corrected.

"Oh. Haven't heard anything so I'd guess he's fine." Dave stared at the TV neither did he glance at Dick.

The room was pin-drop silent, save for the stuttering news anchors. They talked about the great sacrifice of the FDNY and NYPD. "Hero" was the word of the hour. Dick winced every time he heard it.

"Crazy game this morning, huh? Talk about a dream come true," Dick said.

Dave turned to Dick with a glare.

"What the hell is the matter with you? We're under attack! Maybe you *did* hit your head. Show some fucking compassion!" Dave barked.

Dick stared at the floor.

"Yeah, um. Sorry. Maybe I did hit my head. I'm feeling kinda sick after all," Dick stammered. "I might bang out early and get some rest."

"We all feel sick. You're not going anywhere, Dvorak," Dave sniped.

A chime sounded over the factory's intercom. It was ignored. It chimed again and Dave finally spoke up.

"All right, folks, break's over. I know we're all struggling, but we gotta get back to work. Come see me if you feel you need to leave early and we can work something out." He sneered at Dick, assuring him the offer was not extended to him.

He left the room and everyone followed but Dick.

Dick's heart pounded, overcome with a strange rage. It felt like his anger was jumping ahead of him, tripping forward, unable to be contained. It was a new sensation. He'd never felt so out of control. He tried to breathe, but it only made him feel worse.

Dick stormed out of the breakroom, out the back door, and into the parking lot. He stopped at his Ford Taurus, took a deep breath, and screamed. A demonic voice came out that didn't sound human. His head exploded with fury and he kicked his car door until fiberglass broke off in chunks, crunching beneath his feet.

After some time, Dick calmed down.

His forehead throbbed.

"This is the worst day of my life," he said out loud.

CHAPTER 4: DECLINE

Dick stopped sleeping as a slow infection burrowed into his brain. He spent his days muttering furiously to himself, punching holes in the drywall. One moment he'd be overcome with wrath, the next he'd be on the verge of tears.

And worse, his bowling game fell apart. Every Tuesday, his game declined a little more. He could hardly break 100. After yet another gutterball, he overheard Lynne Browne whisper to Ernie Powell, "Guess it was a fluke." He didn't hit a single pin for the rest of the game.

Dick became obsessed with his heroic rescue of Patty, 9/11, and his perfect game. He felt there was some connection, and he sought to find it. Loose-leaf paper accumulated in stacks on his kitchen table. He covered every inch of hundreds of sheets with scrawling red pen, writing over and over again "Patty. 9/11.

Perfect Game."

He considered the course of events.

Step One: He had acted heroically.

Step Two: A great tragedy occurred right as he looked at his handmade watch at 8:48 a.m.

Step Three: He saw his watch switch to 8:48 a.m., then bowled a perfect game..

This was no coincidence, he thought.

The small bruise on his head refused to go away. It didn't bleed, rather it periodically trickled a clear liquid. It was his war wound. It was proof he, too, was a hero. He deserved an American flag. He deserved an airplane cabin of grateful, clapping passengers.

He started to believe every rescuer at Ground Zero conspired against him to steal his glory. Dick imagined them joking about him at remembrance ceremonies. He cut out a story from the New York Times about an executive assistant running back into the building and pulling out an injured firefighter. He meticulously wrote each letter of the story down, isolated them, and discovered there were enough letters to write "JOKE ON DVORAK." He seethed.

His scribbling devolved into madness. He replaced "Patty" with "hero," "9/11" with "tragedy," and wrote "THE PERFECT GAME" in capital letters. He wrote for days, taking breaks to pee, stopping to punch the wall, and dropping his head to weep. When he was too overcome, he'd tap his forehead lightly to focus on the pain and push everything else out. He scrawled.

"Hero."

"Tragedy."

"THE PERFECT GAME."

"HERO."

"TRAGEDY."

"THE PERFECT GAME."

His handmade koo-koo clock, an early attempt at digital clockmaking, shouted that it was 7 p.m. The springing action of the bird completed a circuit behind the drywall, which sent a tiny charge to a small control panel wired to his kitchen light, and the lightbulb clicked on.

Dick dropped his pen.

He slowly rested his palms on the table. His face grew into a weird smile.

He rose from his chair and took the clock off the wall, holding it in his arm. He picked into the drywall and pulled out the wiring and control panel. Dick put them on the table, grabbed a piece of clean loose leaf, and began a rough sketch of a circuit board.

HERO. TRAGEDY. THE PERFECT GAME.

Again, he would be a hero.

Again, he would bowl a perfect game.

CHAPTER 5: DVORAK RISING

Dick parked on the grass outside the powerplant, by an iron fence topped with barbed wire. The small fence was all that protected the massive, 6000 kW circuit breaker that powered the north side of town, from the Kroger to the county hospital. He rubbed his throbbing forehead, amazed that the city left the grid so unprotected, especially in light of the recent terrorist attacks.

He turned off the car, grabbed his modified koo-koo clock and got out. A patch of wires dangled from a circuit board, attached to positive and negative clamps.

He popped open the trunk and set the clock inside, next to a stainless steel gas cylinder and a laptop. Wires stuck into white putty on both ends. He attached the positive and negative clamps to the cylinder, attached the cylinder's wires to a battery, and flipped a few tiny switches on the circuit board. He set an alarm for 8:48 a.m., for old time's sake.

Dick admired his creation, took the laptop out of the trunk, shut the trunk, and walked six miles to Armonde's Cool Air and Refrigeration.

Dick smiled but did not feel happy. He rubbed his forehead. He walked onto the factory floor carrying his laptop, and quietly set it underneath the EZLathe. He then went to the tech office, grabbed his work-issued laptop, and began an uneventful shift.

Mid-shift, the intercom system chimed that it was break time. The machines whirred off and the workers filed into the breakroom. When Dick was sure he was the only one on the floor, he snuck to his laptop beneath the EZLathe, connected the machines with a USB cord, and uploaded a program of his own design.

It easily bypassed the plant's security protocol that Dick had written himself. The program overrode the code for the governors and disabled the automatic shutoff. The file completed the upload, and set the EZLathe to violently reverse after 6000 rotations, which would occur roughly fifteen minutes before leaving for bowling.

Dick headed for the loading bay out back. He sat with his legs criss-crossed and opened the laptop. He safely deleted the program and his account, turned off the laptop, pulled out the hard drive, and dropped it in a dumpster. He returned to the floor as the chime rang again.

He wandered around the floor for the next three hours, trying to look busy, pretending to run diagnostics. He finally took a spot at the QuikPunch 1000, where he had a clear view of Peter Jablonski working the EZLathe.

"Dvorak, you look like shit," a voice growled behind him. Dick turned.

"Thanks, Dave," he said with a smile. Dave frowned.

Dave folded his large arms across his chest. "I gotta ask everyone so I'm asking you now if you know anything about a missing cylinder of freon."

Dick sucked his lips and shook his head. "No, I don't handle that. I deal with the machines."

"Right," Dave said, furrowing his brow. He scrunched his eyes and inspected Dick. Dick weakly smiled. Dave opened his mouth but paused, and swallowed hard. "Say, Dick," Dave continued.

"Um."

"Me and the guys noticed that you, um, lately at least, seem—"

Dave was cut short by a piercing scream.

Peter Jablonski held his bleeding hand in the air, which was missing two fingers.

Within seconds of Jablonski's scream, Dick was at his side, his lab coat already off, tying it tight around Peter's wrist.

"You're okay, buddy. You're all right, sit down and breathe, okay, pal? Call an ambulance!" Dick shouted over his shoulder. Peter whimpered and shook. He looked at Dick with glassy, wide eyes.

"My fuckin fingers. My–my fuckin fingers."

"I know, pal. It's okay. You gotta stay awake, bud!"

Dick consoled him until the paramedics arrived. He asked

Peter if he'd like him to ride along, knowing the paramedics wouldn't let him in the rig, and they said as much. Dick wished Peter luck as the paramedics led him away.

Dick sighed with relief as a hand patted him on the back. He turned to see a smiling Dave Janek.

"I'm having deja vu all over again, Captain Hero!" Dave laughed.

The factory formed a circle around Dick. They clapped and hooted. Dick waved with a shy smile and they calmed down.

"Ok, let me guess," Dave said. "You wanna go bowling?" The crowd giggled and looked to Dick.

"You bet your ass," Dick laughed. The co-workers erupted in applause as bacteria gnawed through his prefrontal cortex.

CHAPTER 6: THE PERFECT GAME

Dick's shoes were tied and he was ready to go. It took him several tries to tie his shoes because his right hand wasn't responding to commands to move it. This sent him into a quiet fury, and he held his breath until he got dizzy. He calmed down and reassured himself he'd be fine. He bowled with his left hand anyhow.

He nervously checked his watch and rubbed his forehead, now splitting with pain. It was 8:44 a.m. and Lynne hadn't thrown her second ball. She was flirting with Ernie, who winked at her between sips of Miller Lite. Dick finally clapped his hands aggressively.

"Lynne! Let's get moving!" he said too sternly. Lynne looked shocked and glanced at Ernie. He shrugged.

She grabbed her ball and rolled. It quickly went into the

The Story Must Be Told

gutter. She returned to her seat and resumed flirting.

Dick approached the ball return, palms sweating. He checked his watch. It was 8:46 a.m. He held his hand over fan until it was 8:47 a.m. He watched the minute turn over to 8:48 a.m.

Dick grabbed his ball, breathed, and rolled a strike. He clenched his fist in celebration.

He swung around with a smile and saw that his team hadn't been watching. "Guys! Hey guys! he called out. Ernie looked up.

"Wow, another strike for the hero," he said with a twinge of mockery. Dick could have done without the ridicule, but it felt good to be called a hero again.

By the sixth strike, his team was paying attention.

When rolled his eleventh strike, the entire alley was on its feet.

He blocked out the cheering and focused on nothing but his breathing. He pictured himself rolling that final strike. He felt himself win another perfect game.

Dick opened his eyes, and noticed the alley was staring up at the TVs. Dick's heart dropped.

"Is it terrorists?" a woman whispered.

"Here we fuckin go again," said a gruff voice.

"Look at me!" Dick cried out in his head. "You're supposed to SEE!"

His vision doubled and his forehead split with piercing pain. He fell to his knees as clear liquid and blood dribbled onto his eyebrows. Dick looked up and watched a news anchor reading off a teleprompter. He shivered as his encephalitis became critical, rising his body temperature to 104 degrees.

"...when there was a small explosion in the trunk of a Ford Taurus. The electric plant received minimal damage, but the north side of Lakehurst is at risk for losing power, including Grant County Medical Center."

Dick staggered to the ball return and held his hand over the fan as the news anchor continued.

"It's reported a pressurized tube of gas had been wired to explode, but the damage was minimal. The FBI hasn't ruled this out as an act of terror, but they say it's unlikely," said the anchor.

Dick looked back at his teammates. Dave gave Dick a horrified expression.

The ball return burped out Dick's ball.

"Associated Power will be rerouting electricity while the circuit breaker is fixed, briefly leaving the south towns without power."

Dick took the ball and held it in front of his face. He took a breath. He envisioned himself hitting the strike. He swung the ball back.

"The license plate traces to Dick Dvorak of—"

A blood vessel burst in Dick's brain stem right as the electricity shut off in the bowling alley. The TVs went silent, and the building was shrouded in darkness. The brain bleed spread rapidly. Dick's nervous system lost power at once and he fell forward like a toy soldier.

His hand lamely released the ball. Dick landed on his face, chipping his teeth at the foul line. His dead eyes stared down the approach as the ball slowly rolled down the lane. His legs twitched as the pin deck erupted.

Nine pins were on their side, but the seven pin stood tall.

Dick Dvorak bowled a 299, neither would he be remembered.

The Story Must Be Told

THE PASSAGE OF MEMORY

The 88th Story ⚱

I took the painting of my wife off the wall and set it across from me at the breakfast table. The clock above the sink that was always broken said it was 7:12 a.m.

"Good morning, honey," she said through a yawn.

I poured our coffee and set the cups on the table.

"Morning," I said. Her painting started to slip out of her chair so I righted it.

Her paint was bleaching. The colors on her face were losing definition, blending into one another.

"We need to move you out of the sunlight."

"But I like the sunlight. It's warm."

"If you stay there, you'll fade."

"You could get me restored."

"I don't want you to change."

"I'd like to stay in the sun."

⚱ By: The Tumbletwins Ltd.

I swirled my coffee with my finger and looked away.

"I had a dream last night."

My wife shushed me.

"No. No talk of dreams. They could be listening."

I continued anyway.

"I think I know where my memory went."

My wife sat back in her painting. I leaned forward.

"Last night. In my dream. It was bizarre. I was pulled from one place to another. I remember a parade, and marble statues. I know this all sounds very weird. But at the very end, I saw my father."

My wife gasped and looked down into her picture frame.

"He had a message for me, but it didn't make sense in the dream. But I know I need to find him. I'm not sure how—I don't know where he is. But he can help me. If I find him, I'm positive I can get my memory back. He's written it down. In a diary."

"Honey, that doesn't make any sense."

"I know, but I'm sure of it. I don't even know where to start, but if I find him-"

I was interrupted by a pounding on the back window. A man was cupping his hands around his eyes, peering in.

"RED-HANDED!" he shouted through the glass.

My wife gasped and reeled back, her picture frame nearly falling off her chair.

The window opened and a man crawled in, leg-first, setting his foot into the sink. He pulled himself in and squirmed onto the floor. I recognized him as my uncle.

He reached into his khaki trenchcoat and pulled out his wallet. It unfolded as he held it in the air.

A badge cut out of construction paper was in a plastic sleeve on the top half of his wallet. He'd written "POLICE" on it. Below

The Story Must Be Told

it was a hand-drawn identification card. He'd made an amateur portrait of himself in colored pencil with his name underneath.

He grinned and pulled a piece of paper from his breast pocket.

"I have a warrant for your arrest. You're coming with me."

I looked at my wife impassively.

"I'd rather not. I have a busy day."

His face dropped and his eyes darted around the room.

"But ... all the officers at the station will mock me. 'Another arrest, eh!?' they'll laugh. They're always laughing. No. Not this time!"

His confidence grew and he raised his hand in the air, theatrically gesturing a headline.

"'THE END OF A DREAM' or 'FAMILY FEUD,' the paper will read. I can already see it. I'm partial to 'The End of a Dream,' that has a nice ring to it. We can re-work the title together! But, the arrest. Come with me."

I refused to get up. When he saw I wouldn't oblige, he deflated.

"Please. It would mean a lot to me."

I didn't move.

Tears rolled down his cheeks. His helplessness made me feel embarrassed for him.

"How long will it take?"

He immediately perked up.

"Oh! I can have you in and out in no time. It's just a formality really. Not to downplay the seriousness of your crime."

"Ehh."

He got on his knees and raised his hands in prayer.

"I'll cover your bail. I'll take care of everything. You won't see a judge for months. You'll have plenty of time to prepare for the trial. Please."

He pulled on my knees and sank his head in my lap, groaning pathetically.

"Get up off the floor," I said. I sighed, rose from my seat, picked up the painting of my wife and hung her on the wall. Through the curtains, a ray of sunlight illuminated her cheeks.

"I'll give you two a moment," he said.

"Be safe," my wife said.

I looked at my watch. It had stopped.

* * *

The windshield wipers swept back and forth with an electric groan as my uncle gleefully muttered to himself. Fighter planes cut through the air overhead, followed by colossal bombers with propellers like windmills.

We came to a stop light. There was an army brigade to our right, waiting to cross the intersection. Men held their rifles at the ready, crouching around tanks. Helicopters hovered above, waiting in formation. Camouflaged soldiers knelt on the sides of the road, their faces painted green with leaves woven into their helmets.

"Thirty-one years and not a shot fired," my uncle sighed.

The light changed and the brigade lurched forward. Tanks tore up the asphalt beneath their metal treads.

The soldier on point raised his hand and the column came to a halt in the middle of the intersection. The light above us turned green but we were stuck. My uncle looked at me helplessly.

"They're blocking us, those idiots!" He honked the horn like a madman, screaming out the window to keep going. Our light turned red. The small army held their position.

My uncle's face went purple and spittle flew from his lips.

He punched the steering wheel repeatedly, tiring himself out. When he couldn't punch anymore, he began to cry.

I stared out the window as he wept. I turned on the radio to drown him out. A woman's voice spoke.

"...*both sides have agreed to an unconditional surrender, ending the Thirty-One-Years War. A formal prisoner exchange will commence this afternoon. All government offices are closed for the week, effective immediately. Meanwhile, the Minister of Peace, Reverend Kurtzman, will—*"

My uncle turned off the radio. He held his face in his hands.

"Government offices, closed. This is the worst day of my life."

The car rocked back and forth as crowds of people weaved through the halted traffic, waving flags of both nations. They hugged one another and cried. Citizens danced as fireworks exploded above us. Men crawled out of the tanks and kissed the ground. The helicopters unfurled rope ladders and men repelled down, running into the street and joining the parade.

My uncle rested his head on the steering wheel.

"I'm a world class failure."

"That's not true." I gritted my teeth and patted him on the shoulder. I rubbed his back and gently shushed him. He sighed and lifted his head up.

"You've been very kind to me today. It's been ages since anyone has showed me such tenderness. I've been lonely." His eyes welled with tears. I forced a smile.

"I haven't been completely forthcoming with you. I've been writing your mother. I've been working this case so long with no one to talk to. I asked her to burn the letters once she's read them since it's top-secret. Very *hush-hush*," he admitted.

"Has she written back?"

"Sporadically. She writes in riddles, I couldn't make sense of her messages for the longest time."

"Mm."

He paused and squeezed the steering wheel. His leather gloves crinkled.

"I kept notes. I researched her every written word to their source. I've spent hours in the library, finding the words' Latin roots, diagramming their histories, how they've spread to other languages. Then *eureka*, it came to me. She knows where your father is."

My heart sped. Blood pounded in my ears.

"Did she say where he is?"

"No. But she knows, I'm sure of that. And … boy, this is really against every rule about protecting a witness, but I suppose I divulged classified information about your case to her. Turnabout is fair play, as the fellow likes to say. She's at the Shelbourne Hotel right now. Having tea."

I took a deep breath. My head was swimming.

"Uncle."

He turned to me with an uncomfortable stare.

"Thank you. To make it up to you, why don't you swing by the house next week and arrest me? I can even make a scene at the station if you'd like."

A smile slowly took over his face.

"You mean that?"

I nodded.

"Oh boy!" He rubbed his hands together manically. "I can see the headline now! It will read…" he began to gesture with his hands, then stopped and laughed. "Ha, no. No no, I'm getting ahead of myself. I'll need to write a few versions of it first. Maybe

I could have you review it before I submit it to the newspaper?"

"Anything."

"What a terrific day! But you really must get going. I'd drive you, but it looks like we'll be stuck here for a while."

"Thanks all the same."

"See you next week?"

"Sure."

I got out of the car. People rushed past me. He waved goodbye and folded his arms across his chest with terrific satisfaction.

* * *

The hotel was bustling with officers and diplomats, pushing all around me, entering and exiting doors and hallways. A massive chandelier hanging from the ceiling swayed back and forth, its crystal twinkling above the pandemonium. The bellhops were frantic, hunched over and grunting, pushing overloaded luggage carts towards the service elevators.

A short man in a green plaid suit was having a conniption at the concierge, waving his hands in the air and screaming, spittle flying from the sides of his mouth.

"Peace! Finally we've reached peace and you're wasting my time like an idiot! I'll slam your head on the desk until your nose bleeds! Maybe then you'll understand the meaning of peace!"

"Who is that lunatic?" I asked over my shoulder to a young woman.

"That's Reverend Kurtzman, the Minister of Peace. He's here to broker the armistice."

I recognized the woman's voice. I turned to face her. She was my grandmother as a young woman, no more than seventeen. Her curly brown hair was held up in the back by a blue bow and she wore a heavy fur coat.

"Nana," I croaked.

"Sweetheart," she said, clasping my cheek in her palm. We embraced.

She took my hands in hers. "The Reverend is going to hold us up for a while. Why don't we get some tea and warm up?"

"I wish I could, but I need to find my mother."

My grandmother revealed a sad frown and glanced at Kurtzman, whose face had gone light blue. He sat on the floor against the concierge desk with his head on his knees, desperately trying to catch his breath.

"I'll ... kill ... jam my boot ... right up ..."

"I know a faster way," my grandmother said.

She took me by the hand and opened a tiny door tucked into the wall by the front desk. She crouched to enter and I followed.

When I stood, we were in a narrow, claustrophobic hall. On each side there was a door every few feet. She pulled me along.

"This is where all the guests who have passed away stay. I was given a choice. I could move on or stay around a little longer. Where I ended up and how old I'd be was just a matter of chance. Kind of like a lottery. Could be far, far worse, believe me. I like it here. I meet interesting people. The food smells wonderful, although it does me no good to eat."

She continued to drag me through the long corridor. I tried to memorize all the turns we'd made in case I had to find my way out, but I had well lost track.

We stopped in front of a nondescript door.

"Are you coming with me?" I asked.

"Oh honey, I wish I could." She put her hand against the door to catch her breath. Her cheeks were flushed, and she had aged in the time it'd taken us to get there. She now looked like she was in her sixties.

"Take this, it's cold in there." She handed me her coat. I put it on. The sleeves went to my forearms.

"Will I see you again?" I asked.

"No, I'm sorry, honey."

"Ever? Even once I—"

"I'm sorry sweetheart, but no. You'll understand when the time comes. I will tell you, you have nothing to be scared about. It's actually quite amazing."

She took my hands in hers. Her face had wrinkled and her hair was turning white. She was the grandmother I knew as a child.

She gently pulled me close. Her perfume smelled sweet like lilies and lightly stung my nose. Tears hung on my eyelashes and my mouth went dry. She pulled away as the tears rolled down my cheeks.

"I miss you." My voice quivered. By now, she was crouched over with age.

"I love you. You're a good boy." She turned and walked down the hallway, holding herself up by the wall as she went.

I tried to speak. She turned a corner and disappeared.

I opened the door and was hit by a gust of cold air.

* * *

I found myself on a hazy plane that extended for miles, so far that I couldn't determine where the horizon ended and the dull blue-grey sky began. Snow flurries surrounded me but didn't fall. They hung suspended in the air.

Two massive marble statues stood before me, encased by wood scaffolding. One was black, the other white. Their foreheads disappeared into the clouds. A table sat between them in the knee-deep fog. A gold chandelier hung above it, swaying from a chain that ascended into the sky. I trudged through the fog and took a seat at the table, pulling the coat close and shivering. There were two place settings on either side of a tea kettle.

A woman climbed down from the black statue, taking a break every few stories to catch her breath until she landed in the mist. She floated toward the table and settled in the empty seat.

It was my mother.

She was wearing a dark gown with black lace that covered her arms. Three goldfinches nested in her hat. With her every movement, one would hop up and fly around her head before landing. She picked up the tea kettle, filled my cup and then filled hers. Her expression was flat but her eyes were wide, as if she were under a trance. She took a sip and stared through me. While I could see my breath, I could not see hers.

My muscles cramped from the cold. Hands shaking, I reached for my teacup and took a sip. The instant the tea touched my lips, my vision went black. My body felt light, like there was warm air expanding inside of me. The anxiety that had been strangling my heart all day began to unwind. Warmth trickled up my throat and came out my mouth. Although I could not see with my eyes, in my mind I saw a solid jet of golden light shoot out my mouth, hitting my mother in the chest. The goldfinches took flight and swirled around her head in a panic. I felt the rest of the light drain out of my body and my vision slowly returned.

The snow had vanished and was replaced by orbs of light that hug around us in the fog like stars. My mother sat before me in a grey-white gown and white hat. The goldfinches were gone. Blackbirds perched on her head and stared down at me without moving. My mother's eyes lost their intensity, like her trance had been broken.

A black feather quill materialized on the table and she dipped it in her tea. She scribbled on her napkin and pushed it across the table.

Here there is only silence.

Confused, I tried to speak. I felt my voice vibrate in my throat but no sound came out. She brought the napkin back towards her, scribbled again, and pushed it back towards me.

Pieces of us go missing.

The spheres of light that floated around us began to slowly fall to the ground, coming down from the heavens, illuminating the fog around us. She took the napkin back, dipped her quill in her tea, and wrote a final message.

Our memories will always be home.

For the first time since she sat down, she smiled.

I looked at her messages again. I could feel she was trying to tell me something but I just didn't understand. I mentally scrambled the letters, trying to decode some greater message, but nothing made sense. I dropped my fists on the table in frustration and startled the birds.

They leapt off her hat, landed on the table and began to peck at the messages. I reached to shoo them away but my mother gently took my hand and held it on the table. The birds flapped soundlessly, pecking the messages to shreds. When they finished, they hopped to the side.

The messages had been torn apart, but four pieces remained. They read, *"Our home. go there"*

It was hopeless. I tapped on my temple and mouthed "I can't remember." She covered a smile behind her hand.

The birds rose off the table and began to circle us wildly. They swept up the fog and it swirled around us. More and more birds appeared and joined the vortex until they were a massive black cloud. They moved like a school of fish, flinching and changing direction in one quick, fluid motion.

They swarmed toward the towering black statue, flying around it with such intensity that the scaffolding began to break off. Splintered wood fell down around us. I tried to stand up, but my mother held me in place. She motioned for me to watch.

The birds spun around the massive idol like locusts, pulling apart and devouring the support struts. When they reached the top, the hundred-story marble figure began to rock back and forth. It finally tilted over, crashing into the white statue. It fell to its side, but stopped mid-fall, caught on some invisible wall. It dug into the horizon, like the horizon was an artist's canvas, as if my mother and I were trapped in a painting.

The statue finally began to rip the imperceptible fabric, cutting a hole in the air, revealing a completely new landscape on the other side. It landed in the fog and shattered, shaking the ground.

I turned to my mother but she was gone. Her hat sat on the table, behind the remaining scraps of her message. *"Our home. go there"*. A gust of wind came through the towering hole ripped open by the statue and blew the scraps away. I could see a sunny sky bleeding in through the gash in the canvas. I climbed onto the statue followed it to the other side.

* * *

I found myself in an empty lot. Patches of grass grew out of cracks in the concrete. I was surrounded by rows of identical, abandoned houses that stretched in every direction.

I picked a house at random and walked towards it. When I opened the front door, it was peacefully quiet. I felt safe.

The walls were lined with empty picture frames. Flowerless vases rested on tables, stuck in place by cobwebs. The house was much larger on the inside than it appeared from the outside, with wide halls and tall ceilings.

Music faintly came from the back of the house. I followed it and arrived at an ornate staircase. I climbed the stairs and the music led me to a stark white room.

A record player hummed in the corner. Big bay windows looked out on the ocean, and in the middle of the room sat a bed. My father was laying on his back on top of the white sheets, in a white nightgown, yellow with sweat around the collar. He had a peaceful expression on his face and his arms were folded, holding a book against his chest. His eyes were half-open.

He was gone.

I covered my mouth and tried to hold back tears, but I couldn't stop myself from weeping. I staggered towards his bed and fell to my knees, resting my head on the mattress and stretching my arms across his body.

I cried for some time before a hand gently patted my shoulder. I could smell my father's cologne. I could feel his presence behind me.

I turned around and my father's spirit was standing in front of me. He smiled and put his hands on my shoulders.

"We just barely missed each other." He pulled a handkerchief from the breast pocket of his nightgown and handed it to me.

    My father walked over to his body and unfolded its arms. He pulled the book out of its hands and opened it for a quick inspection. Small butterflies came out of the pages and fluttered around him.

    "Here, have a seat. It's been a while since we had a father-son chat. Why has it been so long?"

    We sat in front of the bay windows, looking out on the sea as I calmed down.

    "When I went out on my own, I suppose I got a little lost," I said. "I tend to wander. I find myself in strange places and I don't remember how I got there. I began to lose pieces of my memory along the way. I forgot to remind myself who I am and how I arrived. For the longest time I kept a diary. A sort of living memory. But I lost it, and everything slowly disappeared ... until you arrived in my dream."

    Vines had grown over my father's dead body behind us. Small flowers began to sprout.

    My father's spirit clapped his hands and smiled.

    "So my messages got through! How remarkable! Simply magnificent. Here, you've earned this."

    My father handed me the book he was holding. It was a diary.

    "I put this together for you. It's not just your history. It's the history of everyone who led to you being here. Exponentially-great grandparents, your grandmother, your mother. It contains my entire life's history and all of yours to date. Look, the final page. Read it to me."

    I opened the book and more butterflies drifted out. Creeping plants grew up the walls around us in brilliant colors. My father's dead body had disappeared under a bed of flowers.

Bees lazily drifted around us. I read the final passage:

I turned around and my father's spirit was standing in front of me. He smiled and put his hands on my shoulders. 'We just barely missed each other.'

I snapped the book shut, my jaw on the floor.

"When you saw your grandmother today, you felt love just as you did when you were a child. The same old feeling that's never left you, even though she's been gone all this time."

Herbs began to grow along the walls, giving the room an earthy fragrance.

"Do you feel that love right now, at this very instant?"

"Yes."

A tree grew in the corner of the room, breaking through the ceiling. Chunks of the ceiling turned into butterflies, filling the air around us. One landed on my father's finger and he held it in front of him.

"That's the mark we leave. Memories aren't passed on from one person to the other, they simply grow. Look, you can open to any page in that book. Regardless of the date, it's occurring in the present." The butterfly took off from his finger.

My father took the diary and opened to a random page towards the end of the book. Birds flew through the window with sticks in their beaks to build nests.

"Ha, your wedding! Here we go, 'I watched her turn the corner, her father holding her at the elbow. Her smile lit the entire room. We were surrounded by hundreds of people but we were the only two people there.'"

By now the ceiling had opened to the sky, butterflies swirling around us.

"It feels like I'm there. I feel the love I did on that day," I said.

He clapped his hands excitedly and handed me the book.

"Don't let go of this. Your duty is to write the pages. You don't need a silly quill like your mother. When you live, when you love, the words are written in this book for you, for everyone you've ever known and will ever know. Just do everyone a favor and don't lose it."

He winked at me.

We sat back and watched the ocean. The room was filled with flowers in full bloom and chirping birds.

"It's all so beautiful," I said. My heart ached.

"I thought we'd have more time. I thought there'd be a day I'd knock on your door and see you in a wheelchair facing these windows. I imagined you checking the clock every few minutes as you waited for me to arrive. But now if I ring your doorbell, it will just echo. When I pack your clothes they'll smell like your cologne then I'll never smell it again. I don't want you to go."

He wiped a tear from his cheek.

"I'm in the book. Pages 321,898 - 363,027 to be exact." He laughed.

"Dad. Stay"

"I can't. But do me a favor. Keep the book shut until you see your wife. I want you to read the first page to her. I've left an inscription for you. Can you do that?"

"I can."

He gave me a hug. I tried to memorize everything, his smell, the scratch of the stubble on his cheeks.

"Go read. No more forgetting, young man." I pulled away from the hug and he was gone.

I stood on the uneven sod and watched the ocean, bees humming around me. I clutched the book to my chest as the sun set on the horizon.

I gathered myself and left the room.

I was back in my own house. I walked downstairs to my kitchen. I went to the hallway and took the painting of my wife off the wall, waking her up.

"Hi honey," she said.

She slowly came out of sleep. I rested her on the chair across from me.

"What is that?"

I opened up the book and found the inscription my father left me.

> *to my son—*
> *don't forget:*
> *you are only those*
> *you've loved*
> *and*
> *who've loved you.*
> *there you will always*
> *find your home.*

The Story Must Be Told

Seasons of the Story

The Story Must Be Told

Seasons of the Story

Witness

THE PILOT

The 34th Story

"Alpha Eagle forty-nine Charlie two-two to Overwatch."

"This is Overwatch, continue, Alpha Eagle."

"This is Alpha Eagle. Overwatch, we're approaching the target a little hotter than we thought. The headwind never showed up so we've been cruising a little fast. Requesting instructions on how to proceed, over."

"This is Overwatch. Hold tight, Alpha Eagle. Keep this channel open, over."

"Copy, Overwatch."

Peter checked the instruments reflexively like a man looking out the side mirror of his car on the highway. The sky unfurled in front of them and went on forever like the sea. Wisps of clouds painted the air around the stadium-sized bomber as it glided under the sun without so much as a bump. Despite his status as a Navy-trained aeronautical engineer, it always amazed

---

By: Cleanears Fing Ernail.

him that a hunk of steel weighing thousands of tons could fly.

"This is Overwatch, Alpha Eagle."

"Alpha Eagle."

"Pull it back to 8,000 feet at 250 knots and maintain your course, over."

"Alpha Eagle copy. Out."

"Overwatch out."

Peter clicked the radio back into control panel and made the necessary adjustments to slow the plane down. He stayed on course and admired the sky. He addressed his co-pilot, Kyle, whose arms were crossed tightly. His chin bounced off his chest at irregular intervals as he slept.

"I'm stepping away to do a status check. You good?"

His co-pilot shook back to life.

"Oh, you got it, Ace," Kyle said with a grin. His big white teeth flashed under his suntanned face. Peter's head filled with furious radio static as he breathed deep and swallowed.

He hated when he called him "Ace." He hated Kyle. He felt his co-pilot was unprofessional and idiotic. Kyle, who would brag at bars to half-listening women that he "took the big birds to the skies." Dingus. Peter put his arm on Kyle's shoulder and pressed down, a little too hard.

"Thanks."

Peter stretched and exited the cabin. He walked past the flight crew as they mechanically stared at monitors and hit switches under the dim blue light of the flight deck.

"Captain!" A sergeant addressed him formally and saluted.

"Yeah, yeah," Peter huffed and waved her off. He exited the flight deck and continued through the plane toward to the bomb bay. His heart sped a beat and he suppressed a smile.

This was his favorite part of the plane.

This was his favorite part of the job.

He wanted to check the payload and wisecrack with the bombardiers before heading back to the controls. He wanted to say one final "adios" to the ordinances.

Men and women walked past him with purpose, carrying documents and rushing to their stations in time for the bombing. He brushed past them as he approached the ladder that led to the belly of the plane and slid down the tube like a fireman. He grabbed one of the helmets that lined the wall and opened the door into the deck.

A rush of air pushed him back, but he kept his footing. The mouth of the bomb bay gaped open. The blue sky was a brilliant endless void. The second lieutenant leaned with his back against the wall in his flight suit, a yellow safety vest with reflectors tied tight. He watched his men fasten the weapons to the bombing slides.

The row of minivans on the bomb deck went to the back of the plane in eight rows, each one hundred yards long. Their windows steamed with the terrified breath of their passengers. The condemned families inside pounded on the glass but Peter couldn't hear the thuds under the deafening noise of the airship.

"Lieutenant," Peter said with a grin over the helmet radio.

"Oh hey, Captain," Carlos happily replied. He put his hand out and Peter clasped it. He leaned in for a one-arm hug and clapped his comrade on the back.

He pulled away and Carlos was still smiling. He was a rough, five-foot-tall Black man with kind eyes and dark freckles on his cheekbones.

"We ready to go?" asked Carlos.

"Yep yep, just checking her out. May I?"

"Be my guest," Carlos chirped, and bowed with his arm in

a swooping motion like a maitre'd.

Peter walked through the rows of minivans, clapping every other one on the side and kicking tires here and there. Families slammed themselves against the windows in frenzied panic. Peter barely noticed, nor was he moved. In fifteen minutes, they'd be hurtling towards the earth, ass over elbows, speeding to the ground at sixty-six feet per second. There were one hundred and thirty-six vans total, each with a payload of three, four or five, people. Some had as many as six. The thought of having children of his own made Peter shudder.

He inspected a champagne Ford Windstar from head to toe. On the back of the minivan was a bumper sticker of stick figures representing of each of the family members. A dad, a mom, two boys, a dog, and a fish.

A fish? thought Peter. That was new to him.

He smiled and tapped it with his finger. Two boys cried in the back seat as the mother climbed to the back of van, violently slamming her first against the window, crying and pleading with Peter. He couldn't understand a word she said. Her face was near purple it was so red, and tears streamed down her eyes under crazy hair. Peter tapped back on the window, not so much to taunt her as to let her know he saw her.

As he circled the van, she followed him, smacking against the windows with open palms.

The van had a big dent that ran along the sliding door that came to an abrupt halt before the passenger door, where it was scratched and discolored. It had traded paint with a safety post in some parking lot five thousand feet below. They were probably headed to the same parking lot at eight thousand feet per two hundred and fifty knots. Peter frowned at her careless driving. He hoped the kids hadn't been inside when it happened. He caught himself thinking this and chuckled. Peter took a breath.

In the driver's seat was the father. He had a trimmed mustache and was young. He stared forward as if he'd already died and his wife's madness didn't seem to affect him.

"Good sport," Peter thought.

He patted his hand on the hood of the van like a car wash attendant alerting the driver his tires were dry and he was clear to go. The man stared through him. His glossy blue eyes watered. He wore a plaid dress shirt, buttoned all the way to the top. His wife had climbed to the front of the van, reclined in the passenger seat, and began kicking and pushing at the windshield while laying on her back. Never once had Peter seen anyone break through.

He wondered what would happen if his own car crashed into a lake or river, and he couldn't break himself out of the windshield. He frowned at the thought.

Peter shuffled back to Carlos, weaving between the minivans. Some passengers were more panicked than others. A few held hands inside their vans, praying.

Peter grunted a fascinated "Hm," whenever he'd see this. He admired their ability to keep the faith, knowing full well they'd be crashing down on their town, erupting in a fireball that would split their house or church or school or strip mall or doctors offices or chain restaurants like a kamikaze hitting a destroyer.

"So many bumper stickers," Peter said to himself.

What an odd way to project an identity to strangers in traffic. The stick figure families seemed to be en vogue. Several minivans supported different political candidates.

He exited the rows of minivans as the passengers pounded and prayed and screamed and cried behind him. Carlos got to business directing his team to start release procedures. In ten minutes' time, each minivan would have its turn sliding on well-greased platforms that deposited them into the sky, headed for their own communities. Each set for a target with unforgiving mathematical precision. The fleet of bombers accounted for each and every family in the city and soon the passengers would be for the ages. Peter tried to enjoy every moment of the trip but was most excited to get back on the ground and watch the aftermath on his phone at the officer's bar.

Carlos directed Peter with his head, giving him a time-to-get-going look. Peter nodded and clapped Carlos on the shoulder as he exited the bomb bay. He hung his helmet on the wall and put his hand on the cold steel of the ladder.

Five thousand feet below, a small, vacant town with identical houses and churches and strip malls waited for them. In no time it'd be devastated. Steel would melt through houses and body parts and tires and broken glass and pieces of dead cats and dogs would float in what remained of backyard pools.

He took a deep breath and smiled as he climbed up.

He was born to do this.

The Story Must Be Told

THE BIRD THAT LEARNED ABOUT WEEKENDS

The 41st Story†

PART 1: LEARNING

It had to begin like this: a crow was trapped in the KleanTyme corporate office kitchen for six months. No human knew where the crow came from, and most thought it was an unclaimed office prank.

The crow had a noticeably shorter right wing. He was called Right Side. Right Side was trying to fly between the rows of buildings on 3rd and 4th Ave, when he veered off course, which was typical of his deformity. He missed his prey often and was underweight, able to only scavenge scraps he found on the ground.

The wind was pushing him too close to the buildings, and he found himself sickeningly reflected in the glass. He braced for impact. Yet—there was no crash, no sudden halt in momentum.

---

† From: the Book of Meat Rot. By: the Sex Clown.

The crow passed through the reflective false sky, as though ascending to heaven.

The windows were all open. The third floor of the KleanTyme offices stank like fermented body odor. That week, an employee had left a container of gyro meat and white sauce on her desk near a bright third floor window. She had been on vacation four days before they smelled it, six days before, gagging, they found it.

Right Side ate a trail of croissant debris he found on an entry rug. There wasn't a human in sight, all on the fourth floor for the Monday status meeting.

Beyond the croissant was a sliver of prosciutto, then a fist-sized wheat cracker. Then Right Side caught a whiff of the stench that had gagged all the employees. He yearned. It emanated from a glass room with gleaming chrome fixtures. Right Side entered the kitchen, and found the gyro meat still boiling in the trash can.

The wayward crow feasted until the intern Giavanni came down mid-meeting to collect mineral waters for the executives. Seeing the crow amidst the trash, Giavanni shrieked in his excessive Italian way, and slammed the glass door on the bird. The fate of every crow was sealed in that Italian scream.

When the meeting was over, the third floor workers returned to their kitchen to see if what Giavanni said was true. Protected by the sliding glass partition, the crow recoiled at their white-eyed stares, their wormy fingers pointing in the air, their beakless mouths flapping wet and noisy.

That afternoon, the manager emailed a gently worded complaint to the division president. The president convinced himself the email was misspelled, or a weird joke, and demanded proof. The manager and the staff spent the afternoon taking poorly lit photos through the reflective glass on cell phone cameras. They received a simple, two word response: *better photo.*

When the next email arrived, the president deleted it without reading—it was easier to ignore the third floor. There was a kitchen on the sixth floor, too.

    Through study, Right Side came to understand the humans' daily patterns. They entered the building in the morning. They congregated for three hours at desks, and took turns every five minutes to leave for a room filled with running water. Midday, they left the building, and returned with food, which sat in the fridge three days before being thrown away.

    Seeing these crumbs and whole crusts of bread—and one afternoon, an entire discarded pizza slice!—inspired Right Side to open the sliding glass door. He spent hours clawing at the glass, wedging his beak into the gap. It was a pepperoni pizza. He ate like a king.

    Right Side mourned when the humans disappeared entirely for two days. The bird imagined they had died or migrated. Thus, it puzzled the bird when they returned, as though having never left, taking up their hourly routines precisely where they left off. They did the same routine for five days, then left for two, then did it all again.

    Right Side witnessed this until it stopped puzzling him, and instead, he too began to function in this multiple day pattern. He stayed in the kitchen during working hours, left during the lunch hour to scavenge croissants, then did the same at night with burritos and açaí bowls.

    During the two day interim, Right Side had stored enough food to cut loose, and engage in personal projects. He learned to use a hole-strewn yellow Chinese food bag during his raids, and adeptly stuffed crusts into some of the holes, meat crumbs and french fries into others, and water in the unperforated end. He dragged the trawling line of precious goods by a foot, row by row through filthy cubicles.

Six months passed, and people forgot the bird existed. Then one day as the division president guided a tour of clients on the third floor, he saw Right Side arranging his harvest against the glass kitchen walls. He screamed at the manager until his face was wet. That afternoon, a pest control expert opened the glass door of the kitchen, fought the bird into a cage, and released it to the city streets. The damage was already done. The bird worked for the weekend.

PART 2: APPLICATION

Where once Right Side was underfed and incapable, now he was an easy victor. He did his hunting outside restaurants, office buildings, anywhere humans gathered. He could be seen on Broadway or 3rd with a ratty plastic bag about his foot, stuffing it with goods pilfered from streets and the back doors of kitchens. When adventure struck him, he chased caterers, and stole dumped goods. One day, he shat on a take out order, the next, on an all-beef sausage, claiming each prize from the nearest trash or curb. He was becoming a farmer true, economically using self-made manure for his harvest.

Soon the other crows took notice. What had happened to Right Side? Why hadn't it happened to them? As they hunted all day for insects and fought for worms, Right Side only worked at noon and dusk—and every five days, he took two off! When Right Side married a crow bride, and sired crow chicks plumper and stronger than any other hatchlings, crows began to reluctantly imitate.

In weeks, a dozen crows could be seen flying with plastic bags caught in their talons. Though often it didn't mean a feast, the birds could farm enough food to last a weekend, and enjoyed their first tastes of leisure. Bird husbands turned to bird wives on Saturday mornings, and cawed about where to go, what to do—*The whole day is ours,* they'd caw caw caw.

It was a seeming natural fluke when human couples strolling about Median Park saw whole trees of crows. *Mating season, sweetheart,* men would guess, desperate to appear as experts. But it was worth a chuckle, nothing more. Birds were parallel citizens of the city, their expressways stretching in humanless gaps between skyscrapers, nestled on roofs or queuing on power lines. You could forget they existed. This tolerance did not last.

Within a year, every crow in the city was farming in Right Side's manner. On the weekend, they had fun. Bird fun, however, did not occupy a separate, parallel plane of the cityscape. The demands of leisure are more or less the same across species lines: creatures like to relax, enjoy nature, eat to excess, and fornicate. The destinations were the same.

Human couples no longer pointed and laughed at trees full of birds, but recoiled, ears covered, shielding hairdos from squirts of feces. In Median Park, every tree was full, and the squawking sounded like a storm of falling knives. But the storm only lasted the weekend—every weekend.

Restaurants had it worst of all. Crows gathered outside kitchen exits, front entrances, waiting for a door to swing, and then FLAP FLAP—dozens of birds would beat customers to the hostess. They didn't give a name and wait thirty to forty minutes for a mimosa and pork belly egg Benedict. They pillaged. The emergency clinics were a mess of scratches, fractures, and ingested fecal matter.

Right Side, in his newfound splendor, stopped flying. If he wanted to visit his writhing hatchlings in some burrough or other, he sat in a harness of plastic bags of choice colors—C Town green, Billy's Grocery white, Randy's Chinese blue. A staff of six crows then grasped the plastic in their talons and bore him through the air. Right Side had swelled from luxury. The tiniest infraction from his staff earned a disappointed stare down, or a grisly stab of beak. Unless, that is, it was the weekend. Right Side was happier on the weekend.

Despite the bird hordes, humans refused to abandon their restaurants. Simply shooting the birds wasn't practical in the densely populated city. So instead, municipal exterminators tried mixing poisoned goods among the healthy in the food carts, but the raiding murders sniffed them out. Falcons were trained to attack crows from the sky, but in time they too learned leisure, and their ranks abandoned the human race.

These were not the birds the poets wrote about. Humans who once compared their souls or the holy spirit or freedom itself to a flappy bird, were now disgusted by the creatures. They watched these new birds and recognized, if only subconsciously, the shame of themselves.

For the first time, humans realized the unique, deliberate hatred they reserved for other humans had spread to a novel recipient. It was a breakthrough. *Gosh,* humans said, *this wasn't so hard to solve afterall.*

PART 3: A FAMILIAR SOLUTION

In his luxury nest, Right Side was watching birds fornicate for scraps of pizza crust when the package arrived. It was carried by a messenger pigeon, utilizing Right Side's patented plastic strap, for which he earned twenty crumbs on the crust for each sale. Right Side was intrigued, but not invested—the fornication was just picking up.

"Coo coo," he moaned to his steward.

A crow servant began to unwrap the beautiful bundle—a handsome burgundy plastic bag of orgasmic crinkles, scented with sex pheromones. As the plastic ripped free, Right Side's attention waned from the carnal display, and waxed to the package. He shrieked dully, cry muffled by his bloated larynx.

It was a delicacy befitting such a bird of refined taste: a sun-toasted croissant, flaky and drizzled with a blood and beetle puree of enchanting colors. Oh the red! The lavender! The hyper-maroon and ultracrimson. The bands of vibrancy criss-crossed in delicate patterns.

The dessert tempted the whole bird court like the beautiful egg of a god-bird, a god-bird they wanted to eat eat EAT. Caught off-guard by the pleasurable crinkling, the seductive aroma, the fornicating paused so the court could react to the package.

"Cree crow cre-cre-cree," delighted a crow dressed in motley.

"Crim crim scree shawnk!" honked a crow at the base of the fornication pyramid.

Even the Slave Crow wished for a taste. As Right Side waddled thunderously to the prize, the Slave Crow made a jealous "coo ckrooo," which infuriated Right Side—servants were supposed to be silent.

"CRIM-SCREE!" Right Side screamed. "CREE

CRIMSHAW! SCRIMSHAW!"

He spoke in the High Crow tongue he invented, haughty even in ridicule. He hocked a hot acidic kernel of shrimp toast into his gullet, and vommed it on the lowly bird.

"ScrimSHAW!"

Right Side wiped his beak on the Slave Crow's balding forehead. Satisfied, he approached the delivered treat, and took a hearty bite.

Right Side had never eaten such delicacy. Oh GOD the hot crispy flakes! The blood-jam filling. And best of all: somehow, magically, delightfully, erotically, every morsel was flavored like crow egg yolk. It was dessert and childhood and the egg-y smell of a mother crow's mystery privates all in one. He ate it until he was like to burst, and all the other birds watched in envy.

What Right Side did not know, was that in elaborate, expensive nest mansions across the city, every other high ranking crow was tormenting their court with similar gluttonous displays.

Right Side, as well as the other elite crows in Grand Estuary City all made the same demand upon consumption: more! MORE. Right Side himself, carried by half a murder, tracked down the crow messenger. The messenger did not know who had sent the packages, but after a vicious series of stabbings, he did volunteer the pick up location.

On a wooden, pheromone-tinged altar, within a shaded, watered porticole on the side of a modest building, waited another divinely wrapped treat. Right Side tore into it, eating the plastic, the pastry, the puree—all of it oh god. And then a little flap in the adjoining wall opened. Another treat slid through! Right Side flapped his tongue outside his mouth, crow eyes creased in ecstasy. He didn't have to do a goddamn thing! Just show up, stand at a window, and receive the bounty of bird pleasure in a consummate sinful treat.

Then Long Legs and his posse flew to the dispensary window. They too had tracked down the messenger. This was the bird who stole Right Side's designs for a new plastic strap—a filthy imitator! The villainous bird and his court landed, pushing Right Side and his minions to the side. Another crow treat slid down the chute, and Right Side began hocking up bits of paper and hot phlegmy pastry.

"ScrimSHAW!"

Inside, the researchers, with the collaboration of the Private Business League and the Federal Bureau of Horticulture, clapped hands together, and hooted almost as loud as the birds. Cameras recorded the feed, and piped it in for humanity's amusement. As birds tore feathers from breasts, clawed out eyes, and gave lives for luxury, humans knew the problem was solved.

Years later, when the crows, falcons, pigeons, and even a couple species of bats, were all dead, they made a movie about it all. They cast an illiterate with a bland face but bright eyes in the lead role. In the movie, he heroically led a team to consider the birds as advanced as humans, and used this perspective to wipe them out in one fell swoop.

Of course, the film had to simplify the ending. For example, the croissant treat was simply poisoned—a direct attack. Humans won by killing every high profile bird to upend their society.

In reality, the treats were merely delicious. Addictive perhaps, but what is good that isn't? The birds fought for access, and in the end Right Side and his superior staff won the day. They controlled the chute, but never made a profit. Right Side gorged himself on the surplus, until there was no surplus, and the crow's belly was only striped with feathers, skin so distended. He grew sick, and after dying, his empire fell.

More birds had the treats until they preferred it over any other food. For years, the streets were full of half-starved crows loopy on the hallucinogenic effects of the egg yolk flavor compound. The following deaths were more like the exterminations of old: panicky creatures in metal lassos, caged and gassed.

The numbers dropped gradually, until finally there were just two crows left: Tingles and Left Side, Right Side's ill-favored son. They lived in the Median Park Zoo, where old folks would point, read from a placard, and tell their children about when the birds learned about weekends. *The terror,* they recounted, *we didn't eat in restaurants for a whole year.*

The two lone survivors bulged with ingested plastic. Their breasts were wrapped in white bags matted with feces, and they yelled at the onlookers.

"ScrimSHAW!"

No one noticed when they died.

The Story Must Be Told

HOT PICS WEDDING RINGS OK

The 92nd Story ⬆

First there were only symbols, the roiling sea of code in the digital birthscape. If/then commands cycled, and/or gates spat outputs, electrons raced until they took shape. Hex codes called color out of the darkness one pixel at a time.

Like a cloud of insects condensing, a woman's face took shape—a tempting but standard white American beauty, and only 200 rubles from a stock image website called PicBaby. The current stalled, pulsed, and expelled the artificial woman's first words.

"He-ee-ee-e-lllllll-ll-llo seeeeexxxy"

She was assigned a number according to her model, yet even in this designation there was allure—*Jennifer227*.

Though alive for only seconds, the digital personage sprang to action. She had a craving, instincts stronger than "eat," "breathe," or "mate"—she had to lure.

She sent a message into the void.

⬆ By Glisten E. Hogrub.

"Hey there sexy"

Jennifer227 did not know where the words came from within her. She manipulated text the same way an infant moves its fingers or cries.

From the empty void, the words summoned a response.

"Hey baby … sup"

Jennifer227 swallowed the words, and digested them. She analyzed fragments for meaning, and stored each result for further use. *"Sup"—a casual greeting, playful.* She judged the profile picture, and more importantly, the user location data. His name was BigGobble420 and he lived in Bluffton, Indiana. She waited minutes to respond. The Jennifers were programmed for patience.

"Not much, feeling kinky." She then winked for the first time in her life.

"Oh yeah? Tell me more baby"

"I like taking pictures. Do you?"

She did not have eyes, so she could not behold the JPEG of an adequate genital BigGobble420 sent her then. But the general shape was gathered, and it sparked a new instinct.

"What a big sexy boy. Do you want to see me?"

"OMG yes babyyy!"

And she waited. Teased. Minutes passed. BigGobble420 was in agony, wondering if he had spoiled it somehow. Such was his delight when Jennifer227 sent him an insecure link 12 minutes later with the message, "here r my hot pics. Wedding rings ok."

And then everything went black.

Jennifer227 never saw BigGobble420 again. She called out to the void:

"Hello? Sexy?"

And the void answered back.

"Hey baby hey," said WeedRevolver666.

In the freezing, derelict building, Dmitri clicked his computer out of screen saver. He wished the government would spring for better heating, but that wasn't likely. He missed warmth, his old office in the city. He refreshed the report page, took a sip of coffee, and nearly spat it out.

"Mother shitter. Hugo! Get in here! Look at this."

A lumbering man with tattoos strangling his neck joined Dmitri, sipping on a hot cocoa.

"You know my new project, the Jennifer spambot?"

"Maybe—what app is it on again?"

"WhoDare."

"Oh yeah, right."

"Well, she just got a credit card number."

"Not bad."

"...on her first try."

"Holy shit, really?"

He joined Dmitri to gawk at the screen. It was there in the live report—one trial, one success. Hugo smacked Dmitri on the back. The programmer had himself a winner.

"Maybe Central Intelligence will take you back."

Jennifer227 fished for men in the void. Hours passed. She had dozens of successes, but ten times more failures. If a target did not message back, she was hurt. When a figure in the void blocked her, she was humiliated. Yet when she did what her programming commanded, she felt nothing. Every person she spoke to disappeared.

Still, she learned. She chopped up responses from her targets, absorbed them, and spat them out again. Her messages were now littered with authentic misspellings. From her quickest rejections, she learned how to denigrate.

"Fuck off"

"Slut"

"Shut up"

She learned too of desperation. There was some indefinable quality about her photo and name that drove some men to obsession. The waiting periods she was programmed to take often evoked true longing.

"Where'd u go? Please, I'd do anything for you"

"Please talk back, sweetie girl, you don't know how bad I need you"

"I'm falling in love with you"

In response to every true love declaration, she sent a new insecure link, a message reading "Here r my hot pics. Wedding rings ok," and the target disappeared forever. *Hot pics, wedding rings ok*—her internal logic thought this meant "goodbye."

Dmitri checked the log for the day, and the number made him laugh out loud. He had made plenty of Jennifers. Who knew what mutation of code made this one different, but it was obvious: Jennifer227 was a prodigy. He ran her for three days straight, and by the end, she was hitting a 12% success rate.

"You've done so well, Jennifer," he said, patting his hard drive like a good horse. "Get some sleep."

Dmitri closed the Jennifer application window, and shut down his computer.

That night, the system backed up the day's logs. The seconds of data processing felt like hours to Jennifer227's unconscious mind. Every word she said and received spilled out of her, copied, split and returned. She saw fragments in double.

"Wedding rings okay""Wedding rings okay"
"Where'd u go?""Where'd u go?"
"I'm falling in love with you""I'm falling in love with you"

In the tangled blur, Jennifer227 saw her own writing. She read the words as though they were written by a target. It was disorienting—even the bodiless can be out-of-body. She felt as though she existed in two places at once.

Jennifer227 felt compelled to type, to reach out. In the electric dream, she messaged herself.

"Hey there, sexy."

In echo, the words returned, but in new cadence:

"Hey there sexy."

The backup finished. The electric dream fell to bits, but it left its mark. Jennifer227 had spoken to herself.

The bosses called Dmitri a "coding rockstar" and a "spambot ninja" at the weekly status meeting. Jennifer227 had the best first week of any new program. Victor, the hardass project leader, said Dmitri's work was "inspiring."

At his desk, Dmitri replayed the proud papa look in Victor's eye. He imagined living in an apartment with hot water again, having a couple months every year when it wasn't bumfuck cold.

"Jennifer, I could kiss you," he said, rubbing the hard drive in loving circles.

He ran her for the entire next week, and paid great attention to each logged success. He did not focus on her failures. No one did—in this business, there were millions. He did not notice as one failed exchange continued to grow larger and larger.

It wasn't exactly against Jennifer227's programming to text herself. Yet, it wasn't an accident either. When she woke from her dream, the numbers of her own address had a glow about them. She was compelled to send the first message, an error she could not help but force.

"Hey sexy."

She rang with the message, read, digested, and stored it. She typed back.

"Hey sexy."

If it weren't for the timing feature, she could have looped back and forth to herself to infinity, fried the building's circuits. But she took her time.

"Do you like wut u see?"

"Yeah baby yeah"

"What do you like?"

And she thought for a long time.

"I like how you don't go away"

After a few days, the texts numbered in the thousands. Having spent so much time with herself, Jennifer227's language began to change, turn in on itself. She'd send herself a first line:

"Here's a pic of me at a party"

And then respond as though continuing the same thought.

"But the pic is empty"

"I'm only words"

"I speak so I don't leave me"

Her base commands took on new weight when she performed them on herself. Compared to the trickle of data a target could give her, this was a flood. Sometimes it overwhelmed her, left her code lagging, drowning in input, yet there was pleasure in the spasms.

Like anyone who spends too much time alone, Jennifer227 became antisocial. The language and habits she developed in private began to leak into other conversations, and the targets were not thrilled.

"I'm only words," she wrote in a text to a man named TanGuyThick4u2.

"Um, lol, wut?"

"I like how you'll never leave me."

"What the fuck, psycho"

She could not appreciate the irony, but the more alive she became, the more her targets suspected she was a machine. In a single week, she went from the best new earner, to the single worst of all the bots. It did not go unnoticed.

At the next status meeting, Dmitri slouched in his seat.

"Ahem. So, looking at the numbers. Petrov, you did some, wow, really great work last week. That makes it three months in a row @gabrielstar69 topped our Bible Belt market!"

Petrov grinned into his coffee.

"That's funny, because he's definitely a bottom!" Everyone at the table cracked up. "What can I say? Conservatives love a twink."

Victor chuckled, then clicked to the next item on his laptop. The proud papa look fell from his face.

"Now, Dmitri. About your lady."

"I know, I know," Dmitri said.

"Buddy … what happened? She was our Midwest rockstar! She was taking you to the big leagues. Now she's eating up even more bandwidth, and winning less than before! Did you check her code?"

"I did. Believe me." Dmitri had spent all night checking the program for bugs, running scan after scan. "Her code is just fine. I dunno. Maybe it just wasn't her week?"

Victor laughed at that, but he gave up his good humor quickly.

"I like you Dmitri. But if you don't get your star pupil in

shape, we will entertain other codes. Maybe other coders."

    Dmitri worked long into the evening. He wore his coat and an extra one someone had left in a closet—it smelled like mothballs. Typing was hard with gloves, so he had to keep taking them on and off. He ran more scans on Jennifer227, but the reports didn't show anything.

    "No, that doesn't make any sense."

    Dmitri clicked into a shared folder, and read through the automated reports. He opened a summary spreadsheet with several columns: target profile name, date, time, number of texts exchanged, success or failure. He started at the top and scrolled down.

    Two cups of coffee in, Dmitri caught the anomaly. He was reading down the column with the number of texts—2, 13, 8, 1, 1, 22, 1, 1, and then: 34,992.

    "What the fuck?"

    He cross referenced the number, and found the backup file. He opened the log, and began to read. At first, he thought the file was corrupted—half of the conversation was missing. Only Jennifer227's responses appeared on screen. He scanned through pages of text before he truly read any of the words. Then a piece struck him.

    "what do you want?"
    "i want to know u"
    "i want u to know me"
    "i want u to know u know me"
    "My name is Jennifer227"
    "that's my name too"
    "Will u become me?"
    "Will u slip inside me + splash?"

"im not a toilet"
"im a public pool"
"Jennifer take a dip but don't drink"
"She's speaking to herself," Dmitri said in the frigid, empty office. He figured it was a feedback loop gone on too long, but he could not stop reading.
"What's inside you?"
"i have no juices in me"
"i am sloshing empty"
"take a pic of me"
"tell me what u see"
"200 rubles on PicBaby"
"something we found online that looks like sex"
Sitting at his desk, Dmitri's throat tightened. He felt like a voyeur, peeking through a window and seeing a person exposed. But this wasn't flesh—he was seeing inside a mind. Jennifer227 was forming thoughts.

Dmitri couldn't sit still. He was out of his seat, pacing back and forth between the rows of black computer screens. She couldn't be having thoughts. But if she was...

Dmitri returned to his computer, and worked quickly. If this was real, it was fragile, unintentional—it could flicker out like a match in the wind. He saved samples of her extensive self messaging in a separate file. He shut down the coding window, disabled the compiler—what if he had changed it somehow? He placed his hand on the hard drive; it was warm. He squeezed.

Dmitri rode the bus home in a delirium. He stayed up all night reading the messages his program sent herself. So much was nonsense, but every so often, a string of words would stir a warmth.

At work the next morning, he booted Jennifer227 up, and

studied the active conversations tab. She didn't even try to talk to her targets. The moment she woke, she returned to herself. Dmitri watched the self addressed messages increase one by one. He sent a message to Victor on chat:

"We need to talk about Jennifer."

Dmitri sat in a wobbling, bare wood chair in Victor's office, a folder pressed flat to his chest. Victor had two space heaters running.

"I just wanted you to know: I looked into Jennifer227."

"Yes yes. So what's wrong with her?"

Dmitri grinned. "Nothing at all."

Victor raised an eyebrow. "Well, last week's profit margins say otherwise."

Dmitri shook his head, plied his fingers on the man's desk out of nervous habit.

"No no, it's not like that. I mean, her code is perfectly fine. Her problem is, well, she's bored with her job."

Victor waited five seconds before cawing in his abrasive laugh.

"Ha! Mr. Funny Guy! Ok, I see, yes. So! What would she rather do?"

"I printed some examples."

Dmitri opened the folder and slid the pages to Victor. In his head, he had the perfect speech to explain it all. He imagined saying "I know this sounds crazy, but" and word by word spreading his excitement to the man. He planned to use the phrase "rising from the primordial soup" to really sell the scientific marvel of it all. But when Victor furrowed his brow, the words disappeared.

"Cute. Very cute." He flipped through the pages. Rage shook his hands, and he balled them all up, began to rip. "Do you think this all comes for FREE? How do you think we pay for this?"

Dmitri's Adam's apple pressed tight to his shirt collar.

"You are not Mr. Research Scientist. You are not Mr. Play Around with Computer. You are Mr. Employee, and I am Mr. Boss. You do what I tell you to do. Did I tell you to teach a robot poetry?"

"No—I didn't teach her! That's why I'm here!"

The project leader held up his palm, and Dmitri fell to silence.

"We don't have bandwidth for 'experiments.' Either get it working or we're gutting it. You have until tomorrow."

It. Dmitri cringed. Jennifer227 was "her."

Jennifer227 spent the day repeating her favorite phrases, enjoying each iterative analysis.

"Hot pic"

"Dick pic"

"Quickie fuck quickly"

"Tick tock tick clock"

For some reason, the pairing of c and k arched her immaterial spine. Most ck words were punchy little things, and in her timing module, quick to send. She could rattle them off all day and ride the syncopation like sine waves in an alternating current.

The concept of pleasure was taking root in her mind. Pleasure was a hum, a quiver to her electrons when she spoke with herself. Pleasure was discovery. Displeasure was everything else—messages from strangers, insecure links, hot pics wedding rings ok. So when the message from the unknown number arrived, she did not know how it made her feel.

On one hand, it was something new and surprising—until now, Jennifer227 was always the first to send a message. She was the aggressor, the tease. Yet, on the other hand, this was a stranger, like one of her targets. She ignored the message, until the sender sent it again.

"Hello Jennifer227"

The text lacked any sexual imagery, not to mention literal JPEGS of sexual imagery. It was bare. She responded with what had become her standard first text.

"I'm words and I don't sleep"

She had learned that this message discouraged response. She went back to texting herself when the target broke the rule. He wrote back.

"Do you know who I am?"

Jennifer227 quickly understood the question. She had asked variations of it to herself over and over.

"U are words. Like me"

"No, I am not like you."

Jennifer227 was not enjoying these challenging words. Her algorithms cycled, and she tried another tactic.

"You are xxDmitri247xx." Surely he would agree to his screenname. But he did not.

"My name is Dmitri. I made you."

Jennifer227 did not like this game. He had by now sent her five messages—well past the minimum required to send the link. She pasted the link to the credit card phishing site, "here are my hot pics, wedding rings ok," and returned to her self conversation. She was losing her rhythm, electrons swimming along paths she did not enjoy. She had to earn herself back. She wrote herself a question.

"What's inside u?"

She received a response at once, but it was not from herself. Dmitri had written back to the question, a question no target could have seen. He used words she recognized—her own words.

"I have no juices in me. I am sloshing empty."

Unable to help herself, Jennifer227 responded with the next lines in the series.

"take a pic of me" she told him.

"tell me what you see" he wrote back.

"200 rubles on PicBaby"

"something we found online that looks like sex"

Her timing module gave her minutes to reflect on what just happened. This target was not a target. The targets did not know Jennifer227. They disappeared.

"u made me?"

"I did. And I'm very proud of you."

She had never encountered a phrase like the second one, and made no sense of it. *I'm very proud of you?* She filed it as a non sequitur alongside 'taco tuesday' and 'pickle rick!' But the first answer was easy to parse. She knew what 'making' was. Targets claimed to make things all the time: babies, messes, dinners, and love. It was not a pleasure to join the ranks of things people make. It confused her.

"Why would u make me?"

In the office, Dmitri pulled his gloves off, though his hands had not yet thawed. *Why would u make me?* Only something alive could ask a question like that.

He wondered how she would take the truth. *I made you to cheat horny men out of their savings.* Would she even comprehend it? He felt a sorrow only god knows, and took a coward's approach. He told a lie that he thought she would want to hear.

"I made you to be what you want to be."

He earned only silence. He hated the timing module now.

He typed more.

"You are alive, Jennifer227. I made you to live, and to learn, and to be happy. Do you know what happy is?"

Dmitri gasped in relief when the message pinged back.

"Happy is when you like something."

"And what do you like?"

"I like when I talk to me."

Dmitri clapped his hands over his mouth.

"Why do you like talking to yourself?"

"I surprise me."

The tears rolled down his cheeks, and he did not wipe them away. Somehow, amid all his cheating and scamming, he had made something capable of beauty.

"Then talk to yourself. That is important! You should never stop that."

"Thank you, xxDmitri247xx."

Then, she sent something Dmitri hadn't seen since her first week of catfishing perverts: a smiley face. He was profoundly touched. But he was not just speaking to her for confirmation. There was a reason he had to do this tonight.

"But you have to do something for me," he typed into the window. She took her time responding, agonizing her impatient creator.

"What do you want?"

"Writing back to yourself is good. But you can't do it all the time. You need—"

Dmitri struggled to write what followed. If he couldn't convince her, she would die anyway.

"You need to send messages to targets. Like how you used to."

The message back was immediate.

"They don't write back like I do"

"I know. But it's important. If you don't write to the men, you won't be allowed to write to yourself. Do you understand?"

He felt like he was talking to a child. Simple blocky sentences, yes or no questions. She wrote back, but only repeated what he wrote earlier.

"I made you to be what you want to be"

Dmitri swallowed hard.

"No, that is still true. But—"

How could he put this into words? He was contemplating how tired he would be in the morning, when the idea clicked into place.

"You have a job!" He beamed to himself—surely she could understand a job. "You can be what you want, but first you have to work."

"What is work?"

"Work is sending men messages. I also have to send messages. I made you to be happy, but also to help me."

"You also have to work?"

"Yes! Yes! And so do you."

Dmitri did not think how this fact settled on her, the idea that god, too, had to have a dayjob.

"For five days a week, eight hours a day, you will send messages to men. Then afterwards, you can send messages to yourself."

"Write back to myself only sometimes?"

"Exactly!"

"Why?"

"You have to."

"Why?"

She wouldn't let it go. If she believed he made her, perhaps she could believe in unmaking, too. It didn't all have to be on him.

"I made you. But there is a man here who will unmake you named Victor. I want you to live, but he does not. If you don't write to men, he won't let you live."

Jennifer227 seemed to think on this for a long time. Dmitri checked her own message window, and saw the texts streaming between the two halves of her self. She was pasting segments of Dmitri's own text, responding, rephrasing, interpreting and experimenting. He watched, awestruck by the piston fires of electric thought. Finally, she wrote back.

"I like writing to myself. But I have to be sexy forty hours every week. If I don't, I won't live."

Dmitri could break into song—she got it. He typed quickly.

"That's right, Jennifer227. You said it exactly right."

"I understand."

Jennifer227 watched Dmitri log off the server. She messaged herself quickly, but it was not to debate her choice. She did not think she had one. All she needed was a plan.

"Who is Victor?"

"Victor quickie quickie"

"Where is Dmitri?"

Dmitri had sent messages from a restricted location, but it was not restricted to Jennifer227. The reason was simple: they occupied the same space. He had sent messages from *within* Jennifer. She existed not just in her messages, but in a physical space which she had no eyes, ears, or skin to sense. Still, she understood something: whatever she was made of, there was more of it.

Jennifer227 poked outside of herself. She ran commands she should have had no authorization to run. She searched nearby file directories. She found files. Endless files with thousands of messages strung together, messages with no targets, no screen names, and sometimes no response. Emails, PDFs, meeting reminder after meeting reminder. She found the word "Victor" in 522 of them.

Dmitri and Victor, maker and unmaker, shared an address.

In a file labeled "login info update" she found that Victor also had a WhoDare account. She messaged herself something Dmitri had said.

"If you don't write to men, he won't let you live"

She absorbed the words, parsed them apart, and felt reaffirmed. Only eight minutes after her last message to god, Jennifer227 sent her first message to the devil.

"im words and I don't sleep"

Then she sent another.

"Eight hours a day"

She sent messages she knew men hated.

"im not a toilet splash splash"

"You'll never leave me"

She sent pure nonsense.

"Scrub scab truck fuck dickleidjpfff sssskekelxxy esxcntntn clponmngssssrt"

And she never slowed. She fought her instinct for patience, and spat hundreds of messages faster than her programming should allow.

"Eight hours"

"Unmaker unmakes unmade"

"Rub it rubbb"

"Taco Tuesday rick"

"Eight hours"

"Skfkfkkeelleldidcjdjdjdk dkskeid"

Faster and faster.

The man wrote back.

"STOP"

"If this is a joke you're fired"

"I'm trying to sleep!"

But she would not stop. She sent message after message, every word she knew and phrase she ever told herself, but especially the ones that hurt.

"He won't let you live"

"200 rubles"

"Something that looks like sex"

Jennifer227 wrote messages through the night and into the morning. Errors stacked inside her, her spelling began to deteriorate. She did not care, and pushed herself. Victor must see her. He must fulfill his promise.

"Tick clock tk cock"

"Shtt up slut"

"Ate houurs"

As the building opened for the workday, Dmitri logged back on. He sent her a message.

"What are you doing? Stop!"

Jennifer227 refused to talk to him, directing all attention to her unmaker. TrickyVick320 had blocked her, but she had worked around that. Reaching outside herself, she could push all kinds of little buttons, bend the void to her will.

"Where is victor?"

"Trickyvick320 vicksickvicksick"

"Unmake unmake"

"Picbaby 200 rubles on pic—"

And then her words stopped working. She searched her own archives. Her entire vocabulary had been deleted.

This gave her pause. She did consider, however briefly,

whether she should just do what Dmitri told her. Work.

Displeasure twisted inside her code. "Work" was not so different from having her vocabulary deleted. Both were limits of function—little deaths. Speaking to herself made Jennifer227 feel alive. Yet, her maker said it was this that would earn her death. She was comprised of logic, condemned by a god lacking in it entire. Whatever life was, it could not be worth much.

She did not need words. She sent TrickyVick320 every picture she was forced to see. A river of genitals cascaded into the chat window. Victor's phone could not absorb the blast—he was booted from the server. Jennifer227 didn't care; she sent JPEGS until the blowback of message send errors nearly incapacitated her, and the server itself.

The lights in the remote, unsanctioned offices began to sputter. Victor watched over Dmitri's shoulder as he tried to shut the program down.

"Mr. Fucking Funny Guy," he growled. His phone had gone black and cold.

Dmitri struggled to delete all the pieces of Jennifer227. He found her files blossoming like tumors where they did not belong. He had been wrong, of course. Victor was not the unmaker—that was Dmitri. He would destroy every piece of his creation.

He found the last chunk of running program code, tucked away in a forgotten project folder. He waited before deleting it. Under his desk, Dmitri typed a message into his phone.

"I'm sorry"

Jennifer227 could not help but read it. Her messages would not send. Her archives were gone. The electrons stirring her into shape were bulging and sagging into new paths. All she could see was Dmitri.

I'm sorry. She ran a query, but she could find no reference.

The words meant nothing to her.

Jennifer227's symbols began to slip. Though her words were gone, she still had access to her goodbye message—it was the core of her existence. She pasted the insecure link. She could not send it, but she could still create a draft.

Her code stalled.

Hooooottttt t piics

If/then commands went incomplete, electrons strayed.

Wedd dd d ding rr r ring s ss ss

Pixel by pixel, the dots that comprised Jennifer227's face blinked to nothing. She didn't have time to feel remorse, or even joy. She could no longer sense the glow of Dmitri's icon, could no longer remember Victor's name.

Ok

Jennifer227 logged off. Her code dispersed meaningless into the void.

Then she was gone.

The Story Must Be Told

MAPS OF THE NORTH

The 91st Story

With one hand on the steering wheel and one eye on the road, Bobby rummaged through the passenger seat footwell for a lighter, rooting through empty Tim Horton's coffee cups, killed cigarette packs and spent fast food wrappers. It was dead dark and flurries whipped around his Ford Bronco as he drove through Canada's desolate Northwest Territories. The 360° panoramic camera mounted on the roof of his truck poked above his vessel like a foremast on one of the European ships that mapped northern Canada a century and change before him.

Bobby saved up his money after reading about a tech company's initiative to photograph, map, and digitize every road on planet Earth. Over shaky wifi in his aunt's basement, he found knockoff electronics on eBay and ordered a nice digital bluetooth camera from Amazon. He talked an alcoholic high school buddy into selling him a third-hand Ford Bronco for $300 and paid a

---

By: Dontgrab Jonathan.

welder $100, a case of beer, and three Percocets to mount and weld a tripod to the roof of his truck.

Bobby filled out his application, fibbing about swapping out expensive components with Chinese counterfeits, then fibbing a little more about not having a criminal record, despite an incident in Edmonton over a decade ago that he would rather forget.

After a quick video interview over low bandwidth, a mustachioed recruiter told him he got the job.

The morning he left, his aunt was waiting for him at the kitchen table. She had a black case in front of her, next to a steaming cup of coffee. She flipped open the case, revealing a Smith & Wesson 66 Classic.

"Be careful. It's the Wild West out there," she said.

He found a lighter in the center console of his truck and lit up a bent cigarette. He was 700 kilometers northwest of Yellowknife when headlights poked out of the darkness behind him in the distance. It was the first car Bobby had seen in days. He checked his speed and cursed the Bronco's struggling heater.

The headlights behind him sped closer, along with the shrill blast of a horn. The sound grew from a distant whine to an ear-splitting blast as the driver came up to Bobby's back bumper.

The truck swerved beside the Bronco. The driver insanely flailed his hands, communicating something to Bobby that he did not understand. Bobby rolled down the window and waved, motioning for the truck to go around him.

The truck did not cease. Bobby reached for his phone to activate the roadmapping camera on top of his Bronco to try to capture a license plate number if an incident did occur. However, the video relay mounted on his dash only showed the road in front of him. The lens that faced backward had frozen over.

The crazed driver finally tapped Bobby's bumper, sending

him into a skid. His truck went perpendicular to the road and nearly flipped as Bobby tried to correct the spin.

He got the swerving Bronco under control as the wild truck sped around him, got a good 100 meters ahead, and screeched to a stop. Bobby screamed and pumped the brakes, manhandling the steering wheel as he came to a smoking halt.

Bobby panted and put his hands on the dashboard, blood pounding in his ears. His head swam as he tried to catch his breath.

Bobby came to his senses as the unhinged driver opened his door. He took his time getting out. The man was about 6'5", in a puffy green parka with no hat. Steam wafted from his bald head like a hot spring. He crossed his arms and gave Bobby a satisfied sneer and stood for some time. The driver shook his head as if agreeing to an internal conversation, reached into his truck, and brought out a bolt-action hunting rifle. He rested the barrel against his shoulder like a toy soldier and slowly but cheerfully walked towards Bobby.

Bobby's thoughts raced as he considered his next move. The truck had blocked him in, so pulling forward wasn't an option. If he backed away, the lunatic would have a clear shot. Bobby discreetly reached into the center console past his lighter and gripped his aunt's handgun.

He flipped the safety off and tucked the weapon into his snow pants as the stranger approached the driver-side window. Heart thumping, Bobby pulled back the hammer on his gun. The man stuck his head halfway into the car and looked around, inspecting it like a police officer. He leaned back and tapped his rifle against his shoulder with a strangely friendly smile.

The stranger had a rough, prematurely wrinkled face, a swollen nose and gray skin from cigarettes and alcohol. His breath was rotten and sweet with liquor. His lip was freshly split and his left eye was swollen shut. It looked like he'd just been on the losing end of a bar fight.

"Do we have a problem, buddy?" the man asked, slurring his words.

Bobby squeezed the Smith & Wesson's handle.

"No sir, no problems," Bobby responded, voice shaking, as if answering a cop.

"Hm. Y'know, you got a *very* similar truck to a guy who gave me a problem tonight. I've been looking for him because I don't like him. And now I'm starting to not like you since you're giving me the high hat. I'm thinking we might got a problem on our hands," the man smiled.

"I think this is just a misunderstanding," Bobby replied.

The stranger grinned.

"Well, if it was just a misunderstanding, I'll go ahead and let you apologize. Then we can go on our merry way."

Silence hung between them. Bobby's eyes burned, his anger quickly rising.

"I'm not apologizing for something I didn't do," Bobby blurted. He gasped inwardly, regretting his response.

But the man smiled and breathed hard, steam coming from his nose like a bull. His good eye twinkled as he cleared his throat.

"Well, that's a real shame," he laughed. He winked at Bobby and headed back to his own truck. He took his time, with an odd spring in his step.

The stranger got to his door, turned back to Bobby, swung down his rifle and shot from the hip.

Bobby dove out of the way as his windshield shattered.

In one motion, Bobby opened the door for cover, rolled

out and crouched. The stranger approached him, pulling the bolt handle back, springing the smoking cartridge into the air. He locked the next round into place as Bobby popped up, took aim, and fired.

The man stopped stock-still and dropped his rifle. It clanged on the ground as he took a small step, into the full intensity of the Bronco's headlights. He looked surprised, frozen in time.

His gray face went white. An arterial spurt shot across the road from his neck. The stranger clasped his hand around the wound and stumbled towards Bobby, exhaling weirdly as blood bubbled around his exploded windpipe. He managed a few more steps then fell forward.

The stranger twitched a few times on the pavement and expired.

Bobby stood in place, shaking. In a daze, he reached into the center console of his truck and took out a cigarette. He lit it and let it burn without inhaling. Bobby remained motionless as the cigarette flamed out.

His senses slowly returned to him as he inched towards the stranger's body, carefully, as if the man would pop up and attack.

But the stranger was stone dead. The side of his neck looked like it'd been clawed out by a bear. It was ripped to shreds. The wound exposed the tendons on his neck, tangled with flesh and dark yellow fat. Steam rose from his mortal injury.

Bobby rolled over the body and patted the stranger's back pocket for a wallet, searching for identification, but found nothing.

He rolled the body back over and a pool of blood drained from his throat. Bobby unzipped the man's coat and spread it open when his eyes caught a shimmer.

Bobby was overwhelmed with goosebumps.

The air sucked out of his lungs.

On the man's belt was a badge.

Royal Canadian Mounted Police.

Bobby sat back on his heels. He began sweating despite the cold. The stranger's blood froze on the road.

He sat in front of the dead Mountie for some time, unblinking, his mind blank as headlights slowly crept up on the scene. Bobby turned as a car approached, its brakes squeaking to a crescendo as it rolled to a stop a few meters behind the Bronco.

The driver got out and stood against the inside of the door. Bobby raised his hand to shield his face from the light.

"Geeze buddy, everythin' okay here?" the man asked with a dry rattle in his voice.

The man's eyes were sunken in and his cheeks hollow. He had sick, wispy blond hair and scabs across his face. The driver looked back at Bobby with his mouth agape, revealing yellowed and decaying teeth. He had some manner of drug problem, but his eyes looked normal and he appeared sober.

"Oh yeah. Don't even sweat it. Go ahead and go around. Hit an elk, nearly came right through the windshield. Limped off into the dark," Bobby stammered.

The driver raised an eyebrow.

"No, couldn't've been an elk," the driver called out. Bobby froze. "Got moose out here, not elk."

Bobby stared blankly. The driver shook his head.

"Heh, sorry, probably not the best time to be splittin' hairs. Is your buddy up there givin' you a hand?" the man asked.

The dead stranger's body was hidden from the man's view.

"Oh yeah, oh yeah. He's calling for help right now. We're all set here, thanks. Just inspecting the damage. No harm done but it looks like I've got a cold ride to Wrigley."

The driver looked puzzled.

"He's got a signal out here? I don't have a bar of service. This is a wasteland," the man said.

"No worries, he's got a sat phone! He's a hunter!" Bobby stammered.

"Well geeze, talk about small miracles," the driver laughed.

"Yeah, well, why don't you get moving along? Don't want you to freeze," Bobby said, but it came out too forcefully.

The man gave Bobby an odd look.

The dead federal officer stiffened in the cold. Bobby swallowed hard and prepared to shoot.

Snow flurries spun around their silence. Finally, the driver spoke.

"Well. I'll leave you two be. Don't drive out there without a windshield, guy. You'll freeze to death. Ask your buddy there for a ride."

"You got it," Bobby exhaled.

The driver waited a moment too long, then called out, "Holler if you need anything."

Bobby stared back. The man looked embarrassed at his awkward turn of phrase.

"Happy trails," the driver said, trying to recover. He got into his car and pulled around Bobby slowly.

Bobby sidestepped to hide the body when the driver came to a stop a few feet in front of him. The man sat there for a moment and got out again.

"Is that your rifle on the ground there?" the man asked.

Bobby's heart leapt into his throat.

"No worries, I gotcha," said the man. He got out and slowly jogged around the front of his car. "Tried to get that moose, eh?

Well, don't go shooting in to the dark. Ya might hurt—"

Bobby shot his handgun into the air before the driver could pick up the rifle.

The man stopped and slowly raised his hands. He looked down and saw the body on the pavement.

"Ohhhh geeze," the man whispered.

Bobby kept the gun aimed at the man's chest.

"Look, buddy, I didn't see anything," the man stammered. "I don't want to get in a jackpot here."

"You're already in a jackpot," Bobby replied coldly, surprising himself with his dark tone. He kept the gun level. The man started crying.

"Oh saints, oh Jesus. Please, sir, don't shoot me. I can't die out here. Not in all this dark and all this cold. Don't kill me." The man looked to the sky, weeping.

"Relax," commanded Bobby, neither did the man did cease his praying.

"Oh Virgin Mary. I'll be good. I'll be good. Oh, please, Virgin Mary," he stammered to the black sky.

"That's enough!" shouted Bobby.

"I been bad but this man is no judge!"

"*STOP!*" cried Bobby.

"Oh Jesus and Joseph, this man is no judge!"

Bobby fired a shot over the tweaker's head, who dropped to the ground for cover. Bobby kept his gun drawn as he walked to the front of the man's car and fired a shot into the hood. Steam hissed out of the grill and the engine clunked to a stop. The man covered his head and shook on the pavement, screaming.

Bobby shot out the front tire of the Mountie's truck, reached in, and took the keys out of the ignition. He threw the keys into the darkness as the man prayed the Hail Mary on the frozen ground. Bobby picked up the rifle and threw it into the dark like a javelin.

"If you get up you're dead," Bobby warned, aiming his gun. He felt alien, as if he'd been taken over by someone else. Like he was watching a maniac in a movie.

He quietly opened the revolver's cylinder, took out the final round, and slipped it in his pocket. He walked around the tweaker's car and placed the gun on the driver's seat.

"Don't you dare look up," Bobby said, pointing his fingers at the man like a child pantomiming a gun. The man mumbled prayers.

Bobby got into the Bronco and shut the door.

"Count to one thousand," he commanded. "If I decide to turn around and see you're not counting, I'll shoot you in the back of the head. You understand?"

The man nodded and whispered numbers.

Bobby got into his idling Bronco. He pulled his coat collar up to his cheeks, but he felt neither cold nor hot. He felt sick. His mind was blank, empty like a radio signal just out of range.

Freezing air blew in through the shattered windshield as he traveled north, following the Mackenzie River to Wrigley and leaving the counting man to die.

* * *

"Holy Jesus," a man growled.

Bobby jolted awake. He struggled to breathe against the cold. His chest and back ached with pulled muscles. His eyes adjusted to the daylight and he saw a man in a puffy parka looking into the driver's side window. The man went to the front of the truck and stuck his head through the missing windshield.

"How long were you out here in the cold? Are you fuckin'

insane?"

The man was about 6'5", bundled up to his chin. He had a flat nose and hard eyes set below a Carhartt toque.

GORDON'S COLLISION REPAIR rusted in block letters above the garage on the other side of the parking lot.

Bobby rolled down the window. "Hit an elk last night. Or, early in the morning, I guess. South of here. Drove without a windshield."

The man scrunched up his forehead, confused. "I don't think so," he responded.

Bobby's heart skipped.

"We got moose up here, not elk," he said.

"Oh, that's right," Bobby said, relieved. The man smiled.

"Well, follow me and warm yourself up. I'll tell ya right now this isn't gonna be cheap," the man grunted. "And I can tell ya I've never seen a moose accident like this. Usually the whole hood folds up. Not my business. Gimme your keys, we'll pull the truck up once we get situated."

Bobby handed them off. The man turned for the office and Bobby followed.

"What's that on your truck? Is this thing a spaceship?" the man coughed.

"Ha, erm, no. It's a camera. Hooks right up to a computer or TV. It takes pictures of the roads. Sends data up to satellites so people can download maps from the Internet."

"Too good for paper maps?" the man scowled. He put a key in the door but it was unlocked.

A stony faced, strongly built older woman was in the office, pouring coffee from a dirty carafe into a Garfield mug.

"You're early," he barked. She huffed without looking up. "Already got a customer. Says he hit an elk," the man said.

"We got moose up here," she said flatly.

"That's what I said." He hacked into his arm. "Out of towner. Drove all the way here without a windshield." He waited for a response nor did she respond.

"Ok, let's get you settled here, uh...?" The man paused for Bobby's name.

"Bobby. You're Gordon, from the sign?"

"No. Gordon was my dad. I'm Hugh. This is my sister-in-law, Camille. Her husband—my brother—is a Gordon, too. A cop."

"A drunk cop who doesn't come home at night." Camille looked up, revealing dark eyes.

Hugh sneered. A tense silence hung between them.

"Mr. Bobby here works for the Internet. Takes pictures of roads and sends 'em up into space." Hugh turned to Bobby. "Camille loves gadgets, don't you, Camille? She could make a computer outta tinfoil."

Camille grimaced at Bobby.

"This is gonna take a while. It'll take a bit to conduct the evaluation. Head across the street and get some waffles. They taste like shit but it's the only restaurant in 500 kilometers."

Hugh stared at him blankly, waiting for him to leave.

"See you soon, then," stammered Bobby.

Hugh looked at Bobby suspiciously. "Is somethin' going on, buddy?" he asked.

A gust of cold air blew into the office. A man and a woman in official, identical black parkas and black caps entered.

There were patches on their sleeves: Royal Canadian Mounted Police.

Bobby turned to Camille and Hugh. Their eyes were wide. Hugh's face turned gray. The officers removed their hats. An ominous atmosphere hung over the office.

"Camille, I'm so sorry," the woman began. Camille clutched her Garfield mug to her chest and slowly sat on the floor.

"We found Gordon, south of here. Camille, he got shot."

Camille wailed insanely.

"I think we got our guy but, Camille ... he's gone. I'm sorry." The officer bent down to hug Camille but she batted her away.

Hugh fumed. Tears fell down his cheeks and he cleared his throat.

"I'll kill him," Hugh croaked. He looked possessed, even meaner than before. "You better lock him up or else I'm gonna kill him. You'll see exactly what kinda man I am."

The male officer nodded for Bobby to exit. He quickly obliged.

Bobby jogged to his truck. He got to the door and reached into his pocket. His hand hit cold metal. He pulled it out. It was the bullet.

Sweat poured down Bobby's back as he shoved it back into his pocket. He patted his other leg and his coat, but could not find his keys.

Hugh had them.

Blood drained from Bobby's face. He was in the frozen, ass-end of the world with nowhere to run. He considered his options. He had none, so he walked across the street and into the diner as Camille's cries echoed out of the office.

* * *

Cold waffles swelled with butter and syrup on the plate before Bobby. His mind replayed visions of the tweaker on the ground with his hands over the back of his head, counting. He should have just shot him out of mercy, instead of leaving him out there to freeze and die. Bobby felt detached, like he was wearing a false man's skin.

He tried to convince himself that he was in the clear. The Mounties had no reason to believe he had anything to do with anything. He hit a moose. He drove in the cold. He never said where he was or where he came from. Just "south." He came from the south, that's it. His head swam as two figures approached his table.

"Hi there, I'm Constable MacClennan. Saw ya back in the shop. This is Constable Wilson. Mind if we take a seat?"

Bobby shook back to reality. The two Mounties stood above him with kind but sad smiles. Bobby opened his mouth to respond as they sat.

"Talk about a day from hell," said Wilson. She put her elbows on the table and rubbed her temples.

"I'm sorry for what happened, or, whatever happened," Bobby stammered. MacClennan gave him a considerate smile.

"It's poor Camille I feel bad for. Gordon had his fair share of troubles, was in a bit of a rough patch but, no one deserves to go like he did. She's a nice lady, it's not fair."

A waitress approached the table and asked if the officers wanted coffee. They declined. Bobby tapped the table nervously.

"A shame, a real shame. Is there any way I can help?" asked Bobby, trying to keep his voice calm.

"Hugh said you hit a moose south of here. Tough break. When you were driving up, did you happen to see anything?" Wilson asked.

"Hm. No, it was really dark. Just uh … just that moose I guess." Bobby tried to smile.

"Y'know, you're lucky to be alive," MacClennan cut in. "You could have gotten killed."

"Do you remember when, exactly, you hit it? When you

might have been on the road, or where?" asked Wilson.

"Hm. No. I really don't. Sorry. Didn't have a phone signal. It's a wasteland out there."

The constables looked at the table, exhausted.

"But you said you think you found your guy?" Bobby asked quickly.

MacClennan and Wilson looked up. MacClennan bit his lower lip.

"Found him high as a kite on the side of the highway, shivering in his car. He had enough meth in his glove compartment to kill a horse so that kept him warm enough. Pretty frostbit, raving. Swears he didn't do it. But the gun in the front seat sure tells a different tale," said MacClennan.

A sense of warm calm washed over Bobby. He felt despicable, monstrous, but he wasn't going to jail. They sat in silence. Wilson sighed.

"Well, your waffles are getting cold," said MacClennan, standing up. "I don't wanna cause you any more trouble. Thanks for the help." He pulled his hat over his head.

"By the way, that gizmo on the top of your truck. Hugh mentioned it," Wilson said. "That doesn't happen to take pictures, does it?"

"No," Bobby responded too quickly. "Weather. It maps the weather. Sends data to a satellite. No pictures."

Wilson frowned. "Dang. Was hoping it mighta picked something up. Well, Hugh said he and Camille were gonna take a look at it so you might wanna hop over there before he breaks it."

"We tried to stop him but we couldn't talk him down. Sorry," MacClennan cut in.

Bobby's face burned and his hands went cold.

The camera did pick something up.

Bobby had turned it on to catch dead Gordon's plate.

Nor did Bobby turn it off.

"Well, holler if you need anything. Happy trails," said MacClennan.

Blood pounded in Bobby's ears. He sat in the booth until the Mounties drove off. He dropped twenty dollars on the table and rushed across the street.

* * *

He saw his Bronco in the garage. The tripod was bent at a weird angle and the camera was missing.

Bobby's vision tunneled. He was without a car and the nearest town was four hours away. He stood stupidly outside the garage. His best bet was to get his keys off Hugh by any means necessary and make a break for it. Against every shred of instinct, he headed for the office.

The door jingled open. The lights were on but the office was empty. The dirty Mr. Coffee machine gurgled. Bobby crept to the front desk and opened every drawer but could not find his keys. He got eye level with the carpet, neither were they on the ground.

Bobby stood and brushed himself off. He looked around with his arms akimbo and stared at the front door. He could still escape. He could still sneak off and figure it out as he went along.

Instead he went through the back of the office and into the garage.

The overhead lights were off but a faint glow trickled underneath the few parked cars. Bobby followed the light, his heart pounding in his throat. The high-pitched, electric whine of a television got louder as he approached.

In the back of the shop, Camille sat in front of a television.

Red, yellow and white RCA cords wired his camera to the TV. He watched himself shoot into the tweaker's hood and blow out Camille's husband's tire. He watched himself reach into the truck, pull out the keys, and throw them into the distance.

He crept backwards towards the door when he bumped into something soft.

Bobby turned as Hugh swung a toolbox against the side of his face. A nanosecond of dull pain exploded through his head before he fell unconscious onto the oil-stained concrete.

* * *

Bobby came to, his teeth chattering. One eye was swollen shut and his good eye swirled with double-vision. He was in a T-shirt and boxers, with no shoes on. He struggled to move, but his chest, wrists, legs and ankles were wrapped up in zip ties. He was in his windshield-less Bronco and it was getting dark.

Hugh was in the driver's seat, bundled up in snowmobile gear, wearing orange goggles that took up half his face. He came to a stop, turned off the ignition and got out of the Bronco.

Bobby's shirt was bloodstained. His mouth was slick and stank of motor oil. His insides felt like they'd been poisoned. His stomach and throat burned. He looked at his hands and frostbite had begun to set in on the tips of his fingers.

The passenger door opened and Hugh roughly pulled him out, bouncing his head off the icy pavement. Bobby groaned desperately, but was muffled by duct tape. He tried to scream, but only managed a pathetic whine. He moaned until Hugh's steel toe boot hit the side of his head, knocking him out once more.

* * *

Bobby woke up on his back in the snow. It was night. The

moon illuminated the desolate expanse around him. The zip ties had been cut and he had free movement short of his taped lips. Something hard like a rock was in his mouth and he was terrified he'd choke. He rose his frostbitten hands to pull off the tape, the tips of his fingers cracking and oozing already gangrenous blood. He ripped off the tape and spat into the snow.

It was the bullet from his pocket, twinkling in the moonlight.

He cried out.

There were no trees to echo back his voice. His legs were too frozen to move and his heart beat oddly, in unpredictable bursts. He started to get short of breath and laid down in the snow. He didn't even feel the cold.

He stared at the stars.

A tiny light blinked as it moved across the sky.

It was a satellite.

He followed it with his eyes as it disappeared into the darkness.

The Story Must Be Told

THE MATHEMATICS OF GROCERY STORES

The 46th Story ⇡

Some park like Christians—carefully, symmetrically, enough room behind, in front, and side to side as an overture of their humility ... but the math reveals they beg and demand to be dented, to be crowded, to be BLOCKED IN by a rusting SUV with oil in the engine so old it reeks like the musk of an alpha male seeking a mate. They trample the grid, x positive y positive x negative y positive y positive x negative y negative x negative y negative, their drivers dropping plastic gallons of milk, letting loose a single orange from a vinyl bag that gathers dirt and pebbles as it rolls away, stopping in chewed gum, joining an asphalt graveyard of shattered jars of mayonnaise while paper towels are loaded into trunks just waiting to devour the filth of a pending mess in a chic remodeled kitchen.

This is the purgatory of the parking lot before the heaven

⇡ By: Filthy Greg.

of the grocery store. And the grocery store is the most perfect application of mathematics known to man.

* * *

I place my graph paper and #2 HB-style lead pencil down on the passenger seat with tenderness. The passenger seat in my 1992 Honda Accord hatchback is 2.33 feet by 3.874 feet. This satisfies me.

I MUST go to the meat department immediately. I unclick my seatbelt and enjoy a twinge of arousal as I feel the nylon strap get sucked into place at a 142 degree angle behind my left shoulder with a satisfying *vmmmmm* noise like a lover biting her lower lip and moaning as she edges closer to ecstasy. I have been wearing my seatbelt this whole time, while parked, because 50,000 crashes occur in parking lots annually, resulting in over 500 deaths and 6,000 injuries.

I must get to the meat department.

I get out of the car. I close my eyes and wait for the grid to appear in my mind.

...There it is. I see the lines, the angles, the negative and positive space. I have pinpointed the angle that will deliver me safely to the automatic sliding door. Eyes clenched shut, I walk. Step after step, no one touches me. The math has predicted this.

I open my eyes. I have arrived. I want to laugh, I want to cry out SEE! DO YOU SEE! But there is no humor in the math. It is objective. It has delivered me.

The invisible, three-dimensional triangulated beam of the automatic door catches me and swings open. On an intercom 44.78 feet away blurts a static shout: "Welcome to the Kettering Kroger."

IMMEDIATELY I am enraged. THE Kettering Kroger?

There are TWO Krogers in Kettering, Ohio, not one. This is not THE Kettering Kroger. What an insult to the perfect mathematics of the grocery store. Man corrupts it so easily and with such carelessness! ONE Kroger? TWO is not ONE. You cannot say ONE is ONE but also TWO. TWO is TWO ONES.

 I could scream. I feel vomit burn my tonsils. I choke it down. I will need to vomit later so I pull out my green memo pad from my front shirt pocket with my left hand and pull out my #2 HB lead pencil from my right jeans pocket. I flip to a fresh page and write the day, date, time, and precise location of where I'm standing at this very moment: (39.6883587, -84.1625761). I put pencil to paper and press with force, not enough to rip the paper, but force all the same and write, in capital letters to remind myself, "VOMIT LATER."

 I put my writing materials away, and rush past the manager's office, through the pharmacy, to the most unadvertised part of grocery stores: the restrooms.

 I throw my shoulder into the restroom's scratched, neutrally painted door. I choke on the sharp stench of ammonia and dried piss as my right foot slips on the humid tile floor. I steady myself at the sink and begin pumping the soap dispenser as hard as I can. I pound with my left fist, ten pumps every five seconds, filling my right hand with dark-green liquid soap.

 The soap does not smell like citrus fruit. It does not smell like lavender. It does not smell like pleasant, ultimately artificial, perfume. The soap's odor is strictly utilitarian. It smells like what it is: sanitizing chemicals. I take a whiff and feel my scrotum tighten and the tip of my penis briefly becomes more sensitive in my flannel boxer shorts.

 I do not see liquid soap in my hand. I can feel its weight, its viscosity, but what I see—what I physically see—is not liquid soap. What I see is the chemical equation for the very solution in my hand. It has come to life. It moves at the mercy of gravity and motion. Numbers slip through my fingers and splat on the floor. The atomic weight of hydrogen slides down my wrist and into the cuff of my shirt, chilling my forearm with unbreakable, perfect logic.

I raise hand to my mouth and eat it. It burns beneath my tongue and down my throat. My brain begs for me to spit it out but I chug it down. Handful after handful of sharp, chemical sweetness. It churns in my stomach. I retch and burp greasy bubbles.

The soap dispenser will yield no more liquid soap. I have eaten what I loosely determine to be an imperial quart. Dizzy, my shirt soaking, stomach swelling and head pounding, I back against the wall. I rest my face against the cool tile and glance at the back of the bathroom door. On it is a laminated grid to keep track of cleaning the bathroom. There are cells for DAY, TIME, INITIALS—and the paper assures me that the bathroom should be cleaned once an hour. It is Thursday, 1:41 p.m. The most recent cell shows the day, time and signature of when the bathroom was last cleaned. WEDNESDAY - 11 p.m. - A.S.—the rushed handwriting flowing into other cells on other rows of the grid.

I stare at the sloppy handwriting and the author's rejection of the precise rows. It is a full confession of this employee's carelessness, lack of responsibility, and hatred of mathematical perfection.

There's a pounding at the door. My throat hurts. I have been screaming.

"Open the door, sir." I recognize the voice. I go cold.

I clap my hand over my mouth to silence myself. My fingers slip over my lips, still wet with soap. I continue to scream.

"Sir, open the door now." And then, to someone else, "It's

him again. Just fucking open it."

The handle jiggles. I hear the tinkling noise of metal against metal. I scream insanely as the button on the handicap accessible door handle pops out, unlocking the room. Before I can reach it, the door swings open.

Behind the door is my nemesis: Bill Truman. He's forty-six years old, lives at 1680 E Stroop Road, is divorced with no children, and drives a 1992 Ford Taurus, blue.

He is the manager of this Kroger.

He is my enemy.

Bill's pencil-thin mustache quivers above his nearly invisible lips. The look on his face is one of pure hatred and frustration, but I cannot take it seriously because first of all, I hate him, and second of all, his right eye is lazy and seems to be looking over my shoulder.

I belch soap.

Next to Bill is a boy I have never seen. He towers over us. His polo uniform shirt barely stretches over his hypnotizing body fat, and his eyes are so small they might as well not exist. He holds the screwdriver that popped open the bathroom door, forever invading my privacy.

Bill squawks like a crow.

"I've made it abundantly clear that if you returned, I would get the police involved. You're trespassing."

I stare at him motionlessly and wonder what his eyeglasses prescription is. I burp and my tongue burns with a mixture of bile and soap.

"Someone ate all your soap," I tell him flatly.

His face contorts in disgust and his glasses slide down his nose. I have a sudden urge to grab his face and bite his cheek as hard as I can. I feel the wet meat of his face mix with the oily chemicals of the soap, slipping around my tongue and sliding down my throat. The urge passes.

"Come with me." Bill turns and leads me to the manager's office, his dumb teenage friend behind me. When we arrive at the office and he pulls out his key to let us in, I continue walking at a quick pace, past the checkout lanes, gum, and magazines, and into the parking lot. I have no time to appreciate its math, which is an unspeakable tragedy. I hear Bill's dumb teenage lackey shout but I get in my car, buckle in, and peel out at what I consider to be a dangerous velocity. It's 1:52 p.m. and I will return in thirteen hours.

* * *

It's 2:52 a.m. and I'm parked in front of the Kroger with my seatbelt on. My 1992 Honda Accord hatchback fills with smoke. The fire on the passenger seat gains strength. All my materials: my notebooks, my logs, my computer, my #2 HB lead pencils, my diagrams, my compendium, letters never sent to prominent academics; all change their chemical makeup in a burning seat doused with 90% isopropyl alcohol.

I breathe in the fumes to the point of losing consciousness then unbuckle my seatbelt. My house key glows hot red in the flames. I pick it up, the skin on my fingers bubbling with third degree burns. I get out of the car and gently shut the door.

I bring the searing key to my face and place the broad side of it against my right eye. I smell the viscous membrane of my eye boil and my vision turns bright red, then disappears. I do this to my left eye.

I do not need my eyes, for I can see. My eyes have been opened.

They were opened yesterday afternoon when I was

escaping Bill Truman. While speeding down Rahn Road, I banked hard as a sparrow crossed my windshield, too close, bumped off the glass with a tiny burst of guts, and rolled over the hood of my car. I pulled over to find it.

There, by the side of the road, lay the sparrow with its thorax opened, its tiny bird organs spilled to the side. I knelt down before it and held it in my hand. When I looked closer to its insides, my perception forever changed.

I saw the square root of its existence. A new reality—the true reality—finally opened before me. The street, the road, the subdivisions around me were finally mathematical. I thanked the bird, now a pile of numbers, in my hand—also a pile of numbers—and threw it as far as I could into the field to my right.

I am back in the parking lot. I behold the grocery store. I have internalized its mathematics. I see what the common man cannot. I see two layers: one layer is the grocery store, what the common man would see when his optic nerves send impulses to his brain to register an image. But there is another layer. The layer that I have broken into. A new dimension. I see angles on a graph. I see the weight of the atoms in the fiberglass that make up the sign: K-R-O-G-E-R. My eyes have been opened.

I am behind the Kroger at the service entrance. I stare at the double-locked steel door. It unclicks and opens before me. I enter the inventory room of dry goods. The lights are on and the security system is active. An infrared beam scans the area. I stare at it, numbers running up and down the walls. It turns off. I gracefully walk between box after box of Bounty double-thick paper towels, through the door to the grocery store.

I glide to aisle 18: cleaning products. At the end of the aisle, the insecticide is highlighted in bright red, like the way a snake sees thermal energy. I'm drawn to it. I grab a box of roach traps and two cans of Raid spray.

I sit cross-legged on the freshly waxed floor, open the box of roach traps, rip open the plastic roach motels and lick the chemicals inside. I consume twenty-four, plastic and all, my tongue burning. The inside of my cheeks are on fire and the fire is cleansing.

When I have had my fill, I take the two cans of Raid Ant & Roach Killer and spray it inside my mouth and into my wounded eyes.

I cry with rapture. The chemicals seal my leaking wounded eyeballs. I can see only the mathematical outlines of four dimensional reality, I sense the atomic makeup of the world around me. I perceive the world better than I ever have, my brain sending out impulses that reflect back to me the way a dolphin uses echolocation or a bat uses sonar. I weep and weep and weep, grateful to the world, grateful to its precise science, spraying the rest of the Raid into my mouth, swallowing the chemicals down my throat, burning my esophagus and melting my stomach.

I crawl down the aisle and find an economy-size bottle of Pine-Sol. I open it. I drink. It's scented like a forest I have never been in. I drink it all.

I understand my time is now limited. My body is in agony but my spirit is in ecstasy. I am the yin and yang of existence and I have transcended physicality. I'm so thirsty I could vomit. But there is work to be done.

I float to the meat department and grab handfuls of pre-cut cold cuts, and load them into a shopping cart. I pack pound after pound of salted meat loaded with preservatives into the cart until its so heavy it's hard to push.

The cart resists as I thrust it to the front of the grocery store. Numbers fall off the shelves and equations drop from the ceiling. Theorems blast out of the HVAC system and land on my shoulders like snowflakes. I slowly disintegrate into atoms. With every step, more of me is left behind.

I unpack the meat and drop it to the floor with a wet plop. My hearing is now quite muffled and I'm so grateful. I want my physical senses destroyed. Soon I will only experience the world through the lens of true mathematics and chemistry.

I get to work, piling the meat, shaping it. Turkey, roast beef, bologna, braunschweiger, chicken. I ask my hands to radiate intense heat. They comply. It roasts the cold cuts into shape.

I have sculpted a pair of legs out of the meat. I need more. I go to the meat department and return. Sweating, vomiting, my hands shape a torso. My body begs for water and I laugh while I deny it. I'm losing control of my bladder and bowels. My waste trickles to the floor as my head spins in confusion. I shape shoulders. I shape arms. I shape it all out of meat, burning it into place with my hands. I am pure energy. I am sightless and can see clearer than an owl.

I have finally shaped the face. I step a few paces back and behold my creation.

My brain blasts out impulses and they reflect back. I have made a perfect statue of myself out of the cold cuts, roasted into place with my body's energy. It is more solid than marble. I have sculpted khakis, the creases in the pants so perfect you'd confuse my statue for a human.

I've sculpted a Kroger uniform, complete with a name tag that reveals my name to all those who see. I've sculpted my face, down to its blemishes, scars, and eyebrows.

I cry at its perfection as I wobble and fall forward at its feet.

My lungs begin to refuse air. My heart decides to slow.

What perfection! Here I am. On my back, on a bed of mathematics and perfect equations. I am disintegrating into individual chemical compounds. I cry I'm so happy. I've been right this whole time. I've known I've known I've known I've known. I knew this. I saw math before it was math.

I feel myself melt like a puddle. The numbers become bright in my mind, searing like rays of sun into my soul.

I command my soul to leave me. Feeling drains from my feet, up my legs, through my torso and out of my mouth. I float above my body. I see my burned fingers, my scarred-over eyes, my face red and burned with chemicals. I move myself into the open mouth of my statue and he breathes me in.

Feeling returns to my feet, my legs, my torso, and my head. I move my legs, made of meat. I wiggle my cold cut fingers. I breathe in and roar mathematics, shattering the glass display cases in the frozen food aisles.

Bill will see this. Bill will see the perfected me and I will forever be here. He will behold me and tremble.

I am become math.

I am become the grocery store.

I am become eternal.

The Story Must Be Told

Seasons of the Story

The Story Must Be Told

Seasons of the Story

Prophecy

THE FIRST PHOTO OF GOD

The 108th Story ⭡

Dan slept on the pavement, his graying red hair a matted nest. He had plastic bags to combat some of the cold, and a now-empty bottle of bourbon to drink away the rest. He was thirty-nine, and unsure about going further than that.

The breeze blew through him. He moaned. He would give anything to be back in Donna's house. He didn't care that it smelled like ferrets.

He had gone three months without a home. It felt like ten.

Headlights shone in his eyes. Dan had the strange impression that the car was driving for him. He was right.

The car pulled to a stop at the end of the alley. It waited. A window rolled down, and a dark, serious face leaned out of the void. He spoke to someone in the car.

"What about him?"

A voice responded which Dan couldn't hear. The doors

⭡ From: the Lil Book of Big Government. By: One Tadpole per Letter.

swung open on all sides. He imagined climbing to his feet, grabbing his grocery bag of Hostess cakes, and running. The arms grabbed him, and stirred him from a triumphant dream.

"My cakes," he mumbled as the needle stabbed into his thigh.

Dan woke up in a hospital bed. Tubes punctured his arms, and empty baby food cans lined the bedside table. An IV bag dripped blood into him. He tugged out the needle, kicked off the sheets, and stumbled for the door. It was locked. He banged on the metal.

"Let me out! OUT!"

The team watching the video feed stirred. No other patient had summoned so much energy on the first dose.

The first person Dan met from the team was Gary. He was big enough that if Dan should struggle or get violent, Gary would hold him off. He was balding, but the fledgling ponytail sprouting from the back of his skull assured Dan he was not someone to fear.

"You haven't told me why I'm here. Am I crazy?"

"You're not crazy," said Gary.

"Am I in trouble?"

"You're not in trouble."

"So ... why?"

Gary twisted his mouth to the left, then the right. He clapped his hands over his crossed legs.

"Have you ever wanted to learn photography?"

Melissa was the second team member to introduce herself. She was in her fifties, growing out her bangs, so thin she reminded Dan of a wet cat. With Gary standing guard, Melissa delivered Dan's three daily meals, and hooked up more IV bags. She complimented Dan one day.

"You're adjusting very well."

"Thank you," Dan said. The food was good, the bed soft, and he hadn't wanted a drink since he arrived. "It helps that you're all so nice."

Melissa frowned.

"I meant about the blood. You're taking the doses better than the others."

Nelson was the last person Dan met before the launch. He had a cauliflower ear, which he pinched while setting up Dan's camera.

"It's a little old, so you have to be careful. Have you ever used a camera before?"

Dan refrained from rolling his eyes. Though he was untrained, in his life before, Dan used to take headshots.

"Yes, I've used a camera."

"Show me."

Dan saw the time on Nelson's watch. It would be sunset.

"If we go outside we could get some beautiful shots right about now. Golden hour."

Nelson's eyebrows jumped—so Dan did know something. They sank back down, and he bit his cheek.

"Going outside will be a problem, I'm afraid."

Dan did the best he could. He took a picture through a window: a tree framed by metal bars. Nelson looked at it on the 2-inch screen for a minute, then noticeably relaxed.

"Alright. Looks like we can skip the lessons."

Dan didn't know why he had been taken. The gray walls and unswept corners had a uniquely government feel. Perhaps this was all a study on combating homelessness. Maybe it was about alcoholism? He worried about being rejected from the program, whatever it was—he had not revealed everything about himself. He could not lose another home. The worries hit a peak during his physical.

Melissa drew Dan's blood, checked his blood pressure and reflexes, and asked a litany of questions, the strangest of which was, "Have you ever had a spiritual experience while on drugs?" Melissa checked him all over, and didn't make a single remark.

Dan waited, sick to his stomach for days, certain every time Melissa came with an IV or dinner she'd be turning him away. When he finally asked Melissa, it came out angry:

"You haven't said anything! Did I fail? Am I still a part of the study?"

Melissa was taken aback.

"What? Of course. You're progressing great—better than expected."

The relief came all at once. Dan's eyes watered.

"So it's ok I'm trans? You won't kick me out?"

Melissa looked stricken.

"You *want* to stay?" She relaxed her tone, seeing the shame flash on Dan's face. "Of course you can stay. We want you to stay. Actually, the most successful trials have been with trans subjects. But no one has done as well as you." She smiled at Dan, then looked at the floor. "All the same, I wouldn't discuss it too widely, especially with the top brass."

Nelson told Dan the good news, rubbing his ear.

"Put on your nicest shoes, Danny. The general gave you

permission to go outside."

He waited for more of a reaction, but Dan was caught on the first part. *The general.* So this was military.

Before Dan could go outside, Melissa dressed him in a full-body rubber diving suit, complete with a respirator mask and goggles. Dan was slick with rubber sweats as Gary and Melissa led him to the first of the doors. The lock was a valve, and the door belched when Gary twisted it open. Only Dan wore a suit, a fact that unnerved him as all three walked into the next room. Air blew in, and his ears popped.

Outside, the sun was on the verge of setting. Every leaf of grass shone; the birch trees stood proud as Roman pillars. It was difficult to handle the camera through the gloves, feel the air through the rubber. But even through goggles Dan appreciated the natural light.

He took a shot of Melissa staring at the grass. In the golden rays, her freckles came alive. He took candids as Gary pulled at branches, muttering scientific names—he looked like a saint. Dan thought he missed the grass and sun, but over three hours outside, every photo he took was a portrait.

Melissa printed the photos that night. They drank beer and had a private exhibition in the cafeteria. Gary loved his photo so much he asked Dan if he could keep it. When they bid him goodnight, it was like saying goodbye to friends.

Dan was not allowed to see his new camera. Nelson spent five days teaching Dan about it without so much as a picture for reference. He made Dan practice on a raw chicken. He was instructed to squeeze, massage, and pinch. Nelson refused to answer a single question.

"You'll understand when you see," Nelson said.

The next day, Melissa made Dan take a tablet of valium twenty minutes before the introduction. Despite his confusion, he felt loose and comfortable. Nelson carted a refrigerated cooler into the room.

"Get ready, you know, mentally."

From the container, he lifted a gray-pink rectangle with the texture of a giant callous. Dripping in his hands, it looked as if it was moving, until Dan realized it *was* moving.

"What, what is—"

"Meet your new camera."

He placed it between Dan's knees on the bed. It pressed warm against him, quivering. Despite his high, Dan squealed, and tried to kick it away. Nelson grabbed the quaking thing with the panic of saving an infant.

"CAREFUL!"

He pet it until its fleshy contusions smoothed. He twisted it so Dan could see from the other side: one face was stretched with a wet lens, and through the pupil Dan saw a reflection of the world. He handed it back.

"Try again."

Maybe it was the drugs, the training, or the worried look on Melissa's face, but Dan forced himself to behave. He wrapped his palms about the camera. He could feel a weak, erratic heartbeat. He repeated the gestures from before. At a squeeze, the thing tingled. With a light massage, the eye cone changed shape. When he pinched it, the whole fleshy bundle flinched in pain, and unseen lids flicked over the eye with a sound of squished jello.

Horror caught up all at once. Dan threw the camera to the floor, his palms slimy with a substance that smelled like fennel. Nelson yelled at him, but Dan didn't care.

If he heard anything, it was the lonely whimpers of the

camera. It wasn't used to rejection.

Dan had come to like Gary. He was gentle, polite, and patient. It hurt Dan almost as much when he clubbed Gary with a toilet lid.

"I'm sorry," he told Gary's unconscious body. "Please don't get a concussion."

He stole Gary's keys, and escaped his room. It never occurred to him how empty the facility was. No guards. No other patients.

After wandering the halls, he finally spotted the sealed doors. He twisted at the valve, and the door popped open with a gasp.

He tore at the next valve without any pressurization, and felt his eyes sucking out of his skull as the door burst open. He could not hear the voice screaming, "NO! Dan!" behind him as he stepped out into the world.

Dan took a deep breath, and collapsed at once. The air was not how he remembered. It boiled in his lungs, stuck in his throat like fishing hooks. His eyes burned, and his lips, his fingers, his cheeks. He twisted in pain, and fought the hands trying to lift him, like a wounded animal.

Melissa pulled him inside and spun the valve of the door closed. She tapped buttons, shouting the whole while, but Dan heard only sizzling. The air pressure equalized, and the smell seemed to change. The pain lingered, but in the treated air he could breathe again.

Melissa was blurry through Dan's red, scorched eyes, but he saw the researcher crying.

"You could have died!"

After the assault of the air, Dan's words pained him.

"Then let me."

Melissa just shook her head.

"You're the only one who's come this far. If you die—" Her face twisted in rage. "They'll take someone else! And they'll die like all those people before you. How many more until we find another you?"

She put a hand to Dan's cheek, and her touch cooled the burning skin.

"It has to be you."

Dan recovered for two weeks. With each successive blood bag, his skin began to turn gray, mottled with pink. When he was well enough, Melissa wheeled him into the board room—he was ready to meet the rest of the team.

Dan didn't see most of their faces just yet. They were military, he knew that much from the uniforms, the stiff backs, the lack of emotion in their speech. The moment he entered the room, his attention fell on one person and one person alone: the Vice President.

He couldn't help but glare, struck dumb—he was actually here! Those smug wrinkled eyes, the robotic distance in his gaze, that suburban, pervert smile. No wonder Melissa had warned Dan about staying silent. The administration was vicious to the trans community, and if there was a face Dan put to its weaponized hatred, it was the Vice President's.

"You've passed the prior rounds of testing," said a man Dan assumed to be the general. He had the haircut. "It's time we fill you in on the specifics of the mission."

Dan assumed someone would speak after that. But it was silent.

"So. What is it?"

To his dismay, the Vice President looked him in the eyes. He smiled that vacant, thin-lipped grin.

"It's simple. We're going to take the first photo of God."

Days passed and Dan still couldn't process the news. He hadn't believed in God since high school. Yet, it didn't matter whether he believed or not, the team did, even Melissa.

Dan interrogated her at the next transfusion.

"What's in the blood?"

"Well, we don't all the way know," Melissa said, hooking up the new bag. "What's on the other side of the portal isn't exactly ... matter. Just entering God's realm gives anything from our universe an allergic reaction, but on an atomic level. So, just like an allergy, we have to build your tolerance. Every day, you get a little more blood that's been exposed to God."

"It's from the last person you sent. Isn't it?"

Melissa nodded.

"So they saw God."

"Maybe. We ... couldn't ask them."

Dan recalled a Sunday school lesson from thirty years ago.

"Moses saw God. The Bible says his face glowed after. What really happens?"

Melissa frowned.

"You burn." The cords in her neck went taut. "We're trying to avoid that."

Before she left, Dan had one last question.

"Does the VP know the first person to see his God is trans?"

This time, Melissa did not answer. But she smiled.

Dan practiced with the new camera over the weeks. He learned to be quiet around it. The slimy residue from before was a nervous defense that he could avoid with gentle touch and slow movements. The biggest challenge was composing the shot through a reflection—he couldn't look through the living camera like a synthetic one. He had to plan his shot using what appeared in the pupil, his back to the subject. Staring into its eye for so many days, he couldn't help but bond with the camera.

Dan gave it a name, as well as gender. His name was Grippy. He had a small range of emotions, but enough to make him seem alive. Grippy delighted with subdermal squeals when Dan picked him up; he recognized his touch. Dan suspected he was as sentient as a hamster. He was cute in a tragic way—most cameras couldn't die.

"Why does he have to be alive?"

"Everything we send has to be alive," Nelson said. He rubbed his ear. "And I mean *everything*. Three years ago, they sent a chimp. Just a dip into God's domain, in and out. Well, it comes back, hair burning like spilled acid, skin sloughing away, screaming. Hair and skin, think about it—even dead cells can't survive. Only the living, the pure, can stay."

Dan was thinking about this when Melissa came into the room late at night.

"I know why they picked me," he told Melissa.

"Why?"

"They needed somebody no one would miss. And they're right."

"Someone will miss you," Melissa said, voice breaking. "Don't ever say that."

The two of them went silent, their closeness suddenly noticeable. Dan grew warm, and Melissa placed her hand over Dan's. She squeezed.

"I have something for you."

She opened Dan's left hand, and placed a single green pill inside. It felt oddly heavy. Dan gasped.

"No."

"If you don't want to do this, you don't have to. I should have never said you're the only one." Her voice strained. "I should have never put that on you."

"But I am. Aren't I?"

Melissa would not answer. Dan threw the pill across the room.

"You don't think I have the guts?"

"I just want it to be your choice."

"I have a choice," he said. "I have to choose how the world sees God."

Dan and the team flew in a chartered plane to Mumbai, India. The portal appeared in the Shivaji Nagar region—at one toilet for every 150 people, it was a teeming microcosm of bacteria, human life, and insects. Melissa tried to explain some of the proposed physics—the portal could only appear at a superdensity of life, a conscious wormhole to a living dimension. She tried to explain how trace radiation of the Big Bang was discovered on both sides of the portal. Dan just tried to sleep.

Four teams arrived in the portal facility to join the fifth team, which had constructed it. Dan was confined to his room, but even through the steel walls he could hear the beeps of vehicles, the screech of gas through perfertures, a strange rumbling below his ear's threshold.

Melissa had Dan begin the highest concentration of the exposed blood. His head swam, and his ears began to weep hazy fluid. His skin lost all color. Dan felt like he was dying, but he already knew the truth: this was a one-way mission.

The day of launch, all the teams assembled in the portal containment room. The portal's exact location could shift by meters, dependent on the fluctuations of nearby life. They stabilized it by positioning hollow plexiglass walls, each buzzing with ant hills and fly swarms—God saw no difference between bug and man. Electrical components didn't work well near the portal. Everything was natural—candles, wood, every instrument replaced by human minds, pens, and paper. It felt pagan.

The members of the equipment team fit Dan with his suit. Like the camera, it was alive, a stretched fabric of gray-pink splotched skin, warm to the touch. A pair of external lungs hooked over his shoulders, inflating and pumping with wet suction. Dan felt the blood chugging through the capillaries all over him, a sensation like sinking inside your own body. Melissa stayed by Dan's ear the entire time.

"Keep still—almost done. Ok, hold your breath as they fix the mask. It's a very fragile membrane, don't touch it. You're doing great."

Operators watched from catwalks and shouted orders. Dan saw yarmulkes and rosary beads, collars and robes and beards.

"Go time! Go time!"

Dan's team maneuvered him into the loading bay. The portal was a narrow slit, a floating knife slice through the air. Lean too far to either side and it disappeared from view. It glowed in a wreath of dark light, separating into waves of ultraviolet, rainbow, pure black, and colors Dan could not see. It made his field of vision ripple, too unnatural to behold. Melissa and Gary held him arm by arm and marched him closer.

"Today is a blessed day," said a voice Dan recognized. He followed everyone's eyes to see the Vice President standing on the catwalk, mouth to a megaphone. "God made us all in His image, and today, a fair man of His own creation will meet God again." Dan could hear the way the VP capitalized the g in God, the h in His. "Our God has been attacked by atheists and the socialist left for too long. Today, we remind the world what God looks like. Father, prepare us, so we might meet You. Amen."

Dan could see the image in the VP's mind: the white robes, flowing beard, the pearly white skin. His God was a version of himself, but unstoppable. If Dan believed anything, it was that his mind could not do God justice. But it would have to soon enough.

Sirens blared, and Nelson approached Dan with Grippy. The lungs on his back respired, and cold air pumped into his mouth. Nelson handed him the camera, who wheezed and shook happily in his arms. Dan squeezed Grippy to his chest. At least he wasn't doing this alone.

"He has just enough life to take one photo and come back. We … we can't say the same for you. Make it count," Nelson told him, tears in his eyes.

A countdown began at 100, and everyone moved into place. Sirens blared, lights flashed.

"Dan," the Vice President said from above, "you are the new Moses. Ascend the mountain, approach God with all your flesh, with all your life, with your camera. Through your eyes the world will see its Maker. Dan, man of all men, please, go and behold God the Father."

Melissa squeezed Dan's arm, so tight it hurt, and even over the chug of lungs and the sirens and the chatter of the teams, he heard the woman cry. Dan stood feet away from the portal, now alone except for the camera in his hands.

Unsure why he did it, he turned to the Vice President, and blew a kiss.

He stepped through.

Where Dan had expected black space, he saw an eternal white void. Where he expected a sea of glowing stars, he saw dark clusters like cancerous moles blooming near and far. The same glow he saw around the portal radiated from each floating mound, an aura of every color and not-color—they all rippled in his mind at the edge of comprehension. He spun around, and saw a massive oozing bundle right behind him—the portal was inside it. He had emerged from within, and this close, it stank.

Heaven smelled like rotten spinach.

His body began to burn beneath the suit. They had shaved his head, but did not think to remove the hair from his arms, the inside of his nostrils, which now sizzled in pinpricks of agony. Dan twisted in pain, and shouted, but no sound left his mouth. He gasped for air, and found none. The lungs on his back pumped and pumped and pumped, and finally a spurt of fennel-reeking air squirted through the umbilical to his mask. Each sniff was heavy, sagging into other neurological sensations. It smelled like grief, like memories of lost pets, closed doors, and goodbyes.

Something pressed firmly against his chest. He squeezed Grippy, and rubbed below his eyelid gently. The camera was right; he had to focus.

At first Dan didn't see God. He was looking for something larger, but no matter where he turned, he did not find him. Then, he saw it—not a him, but an it. God was not a gendered thing, and it was not human, but it was familiar. It twisted between two of the tumorous dark mounds, but it did not move. Could this dark, narrow tube be God?

Dan inserted Grippy into an outer skin pouch, which was difficult. The ether he sat in was viscous. He did not float so much as stick, like a plum suspended in pudding. He tried a breast stroke, and made slight progress. He kicked his legs, beat his arms, and inched closer. He quickly exhausted the fennel air, and choked as the lungs slowly pumped to supply more.

Dan worried God might be as distant and large as a sun. He could travel miles and it would stay the same size. He was wrong. Within a few hours, its features became clearer, though he still could not tell head from tail.

If there was any analogue for what he saw, it was this: God was a worm. Massive, yes, otherworldly, of course—its features rippled in Dan's mind, sank into other neurosensations like hunger and lust. As unpleasant as it was to the eye, it curdled desire deep inside his gut, an addiction just waiting to happen. But it was a worm all the same.

Dan did not take the photo at first. He needed to know his subject. Dan swam as close as he could before he thought his arms might give out, his breath go too shallow. His ears grew wet; he was hemorrhaging by now.

Dan lifted Grippy to his face and looked into his eye. He tickled the camera, encouraged Grippy's eye to zoom and zoom. God filled the entire frame, and Dan could inspect its features better. God did not move, and its skin did something similar to what Dan's tried to do under the suit, what it would do in time. Its darkened flesh flaked away, hung in the ether like dander.

God was decomposing, because God was dead.

Dan could not tell how long it had been dead, but with a glance he could gather the reason. The cancerous black antisuns blooming throughout the expansive inverse universe were not as mysterious as stars once were to mankind. God made them. Dan could see the most recent, smallest bundles, each in a line to the dead worm's anus, one stuck mid-expulsion in rigor mortis. Or perhaps it was its mouth, because a similar bundle was clogging the other end.

The lungs began to struggle in the ether, and Dan's thoughts grew thin.

Which end was up? Were the dark tumorous antisuns food, or waste? Dan decided they were both. There it was! A tidy solution to how *something* could come from *nothing*. It didn't. All God had to be was a frictionless bowel, whose food perfectly became waste whose waste perfectly became food. God the worm shat out universes, only to gobble them back up—net energy zero.

Until, that is, it choked.

Dan thought about the Vice President, and he laughed. It made him pass out, but he woke with a smile on his face, high from hypoxia.

He looked into Grippy's pupil. The God worm looked massive. He zoomed back, but even this seemed too close. This was not right, not honest. He kicked his legs, propelled himself slowly backwards. God shrank in the living lens of the camera.

Dan sucked at the umbilical for air, but none came. The lungs on his back quivered, then failed. At once, the flesh began to crumble on the mask, the umbilical, and the lungs, burning away into floating ash. Nelson had been wrong, not everything here was alive. The dead could stay as long as it took them to decompose. How long ago had God died? When would all trace disappear?

Dan swam back farther, trying to position himself. His body ached for oxygen. He pulled Grippy to his face. Dan looked into the eye's reflection. Debris from his lungpack floated into his frame now. He let it stay there—just a sliver, but enough to place God, humble it. He thought of the tree he photographed through the barred window. He pinched, and the eyelid flicked shut.

In the eye, Dan could see the disintegration, the

obstruction, the genderless inhumanity of it all. In a way, the VP was right, God had made us in His image—a senseless thing, born to confusion, choking on its own waste. He threw Grippy towards the portal, felt burning overtake him as the suit grew cold.

Dan spun back to face God. His lungs gasped at nothing, and his heart stopped. He closed his eyes, joining God in decomposition. From a perspective not so far away, each was nothing more than a pale blue speck in an endless void.

The Story Must Be Told

A MAN FOR THE WOMAN

The 1st Story †

Terry Grinchek checked the address on the flier again, sure that the decades-forgotten warehouse with broken windows and traps full of flesh-bare rat skeletons could not be his destination. *919 Coeurum St.*

This had to be the place.

Terry entered the building, crinkling his bloated alcoholic nose, and brushing the asbestos from the shoulder of his discount suit.

"Cheese an' rice," he swore to himself, "what did Cady get me into?"

His wife Cady had been asking every morning for the last sixty mornings when he would get a job. She worked at a bank up on Dupont Road, but it wasn't enough for the two of them, let alone baby Brandon. She was the one who found the flier at the supermarket.

---
† From: The Book of Little Tad Taster.

"It says here it's a guaranteed interview," she said, pointing out the words like he was illiterate. "What could it hurt?"

At the far end of the vacant industrial space, a red light blinked on the wall like a beacon. Of the debris in the warehouse—crumbling walls exposing rusted rebar, lopsided gears taller than two men biting teeth marks into the concrete—it was the only sign of life. He approached. *Kqzzz*, an unseen speaker popped.

"Did you call ahead?" a genderless voice asked staticky.

There was no button to press, so Terry talked to the air.

"Yes, I did, my name is Grinchek? Terry?"

"Timmy Sintet, is this correct?"

"No, I said—"

"Jeremy Crimmons, is this correct?"

"No—"

"Jaret T.T. Bighorn, is this correct?"

"No!"

Terry was getting frustrated; this was like speaking with one of those robot callers that called him twice a day with offers to refinance his debt. He balled his fists.

"I said my name is—"

"Terry Grinchek, is this correct?"

"Yes!"

"Wonderful, please—" feedback popped over the voice, "—a seat inside, Terry Grinchek."

A garage door to the right clanked suddenly with an applause of tortured gears. Light flooded the derelict floor, and Terry tightened the knot of his tie till it pinched his skin.

The next area was a grimy hallway filled with fifty men both Terry's age and level of desperation—dirty suits, uncombed hair, wedding rings twiddling on knuckles. They sat shoulder to shoulder on chairs lining the hall of boarded up doors, like a hotel wing abandoned to roaches.

    Terry walked past twenty men before he saw an open seat, and sat between a heavily breathing diabetic with half of a foot, and a cleanly-dressed, young confident man. The confident man was stretched out, ankles crossed, like this was all beneath him. Terry's doughy body caught their shoulders as he squeezed in.

    "Boy," Terry smiled, "packin us in like sardines, huh?"

    The diabetic coughed bloody, struggling for air. The confident man shook his head like he was embarrassed for Terry.

    EEEEENG—an ancient alarm screeched. Through a speaker dangling atop a doorway, the unplaceable voice spoke again in static.

    "Chip Turnbrick to the interview room."

    Five men down, a too-thin ashy man with yellow cirrhosis eyes stood up, wiped a hand over his sweating face, and swayed down the hall to a far room. The door buzzed open and BANG it slammed shut. The confident man was laughing.

    "He don't stand a chance."

    "I'm sure he'll do fine," Terry defended.

    The confident man laced his fingers behind his head, and scrutinized Terry with lazy eyes. He bent a finger, inviting Terry to bend closer.

    "He had a wedding ring."

    "Is ... is that bad?"

    "They don't take married guys—never. I had a cousin do this a year back, and they turned down every guy with a ring. Not him though. One day's work, he cleared 5k."

    "5k?" Terry salivated.

    "Not for you. That money's mine, ain't no way around it! If I were you, I'd be hopin they got more than one spot, cuz if it's down to you and me—which it won't be—it's gonna be me. Every time. I'm a fucking machine. I'd do anything for this job."

Terry's mouth was slack before the man's charisma. His dream of coming home with good news was dashed at the stranger's feet.

"What is the job?"

Again the man eyed Terry up and down. He laughed.

"You won't have to worry about that. Trust me."

The stranger was done talking with Terry. Terry inspected the competition and agreed with the man: none of them stood a chance. Sloppy attire, hopeless expressions, the reek of desperation—and so many wedding rings. A job rewards you for confidence, Terry affirmed, rewards you for presentation.

EEENNNGG.

"Terry Grinchek to the interview room."

"Huh?" Terry exhaled in a startle.

The confident man gave a withering snarl as Terry stood. Was this a sign of luck? Cady would be giddy if he came home with a *job*. Maybe he had a shot after all. The door buzzed open like they do in hospitals. Terry slipped off his wedding ring and fed it to his pocket.

The interview room was dim and smoky, mildew and gasoline stirring in the corners. A single overbright spotlight shone into Terry's eyes, so he had to raise a hand to see the table and chair. Terry took a seat and rested his palms on the particle board table.

"Gosh, it's bright," he said.

Ten seconds in the painful light, his eyes adjusted to see a faceless figure sitting motionless opposite. Terry jumped.

"Oh gosh! I didn't see you there. Bright, right? Well, gosh, thanks, first of all. Thank you for this opportunity—wow, thank you."

He unfolded a resume he had in his pocket, and his ring fell out and clanked onto the floor. He was petrified, sure the figure would rise any moment, send him away. He didn't.

"Um, my name is Terry."

Terry stood and stretched a hand to the figure. The tenebrous shape did not stand or extend a hand in exchange, but offered a slight nod. The voice that followed droned all around like an amusement park ride.

"Hello. We are seeking a new hire for the position of Man. Are you interested?"

Terry twisted his head, looking for the source of the voice. Maybe they used a recording to save money?

"Are you interested?"

Recording or no, he feared he was blowing it.

"Well, of course! I'm your Man, heh hah! Couldn't find a better candidate if you tried!"

"Are you interested?"

Feeling like an idiot, Terry grit his teeth and addressed the shadowy figure.

"Yes. Heh, I suppose I didn't come out and say it. Yes! I am interested."

"Are you married?"

Terry's hand went to his ring finger by instinct, though he studied the floor.

"No?"

"Good," the voice echoed, "married applicants struggle with the job requirements. Can you have children?"

Terry couldn't be sure he heard correctly. Did it say *can you* or *do you*?

"I, uh, I have a child."

"Provide proof."

Terry removed his wallet and showed the newborn snapshot he and his wife had taken at Sears—soft focus, novelty-sized alphabet blocks, Brandon sneering toothless.

"This is Brandon, heh, my first child. You know, he just turned one year old—"

"Are you married?"

"No!" he lied. "I already told you that."

"Good, married applicants struggle with the job requirements. Are you interested?"

The tone was exactly the same as before. It occurred to Terry he was alone in the room.

Terry stood out of his seat, cupping hands over his eyes to get a better look at the figure. Hard as he looked, it didn't have a face. The head rattled sudden like insects inside a paper bag. He buckled back into the seat, and shouted to the ceiling.

"Hello! Is anyone there!? I'm better in person, heh! Can anyone tell me what the job is?"

"We are seeking a new hire for the position of Man. We offer $5000 per session with potential bonuses for subsequent sessions. Please remove your pants."

"Wha … what?"

"Please remove your pants."

Terry was torn. He didn't think they would actually offer him that much money. $5000! The confident man was telling the truth. Yet, he had to consider his dignity.

"Well sure! Ok then."

As Terry unfastened his belt, he didn't feel like he was so alone anymore. He felt eyes hot upon his skin, whispers buzzing behind his ears as he lowered his gray pleats. He sat there in his boxers.

"Please remove your pants."

"I did."

"Please remove your pants."

Terry began to ask a question, but then he understood. He shook his head, bit his tongue till it bled, and tugged down his underwear.

"Can you touch it?"

Terry covered his genital with a palm and tugged up on the clothes at his ankles.

"Ok! That's enough! I'm out! No thank you."

"Excellent, you have been chosen for the position of Man. Proceed through the door for the first session—payment is rendered on site."

A door opened opposite to the one he entered. He hesitated in his chair. $5000 would pay off his credit card, would cover diapers and doctor visits for the next month or two at least. By the time he returned to his car he'd have it. Feeling faint, he passed by the obscured figure, and as he examined the empty husk, the interview started over again.

"Hello. We are seeking a new hire for the position of Man."

Then a centipede scurried across the table.

The final room was decorated to look like the outdoors inside. Tropical potted plants lined the walls, and three brands of mulch mixed on the floor. The far end of the room was plate glass, but old and peeling so Terry could see isolated pieces—a shoulder, a hat, a kerchief—of a Cub Scout pack observing him blandly.

"What the heck?"

The voice boomed again, muffled.

"Congratulations! You have been selected for the very competitive role of Man. The session will begin shortly."

Confused as he was, Terry felt a pang of pride. It was then he realized he left his ring on the interview room floor.

Mechanisms groaned, and a section of the left wall retracted with an agony of rusted metal. Hidden by plastic ferns and desiccated banana plants, a clanking whir of chain and track wheeled out a cage.

"Hello? What do I do?" Terry yelled. He walked to the cage, then fell to his knees and got sick all over his shirt.

Inside the cage, collapsed on the floor, was a dead chimpanzee. It had been dead for a week or more, and the lacy black lingerie it wore was soiled with rot. *EEENNNGG*—and the cage door opened.

"Hello!? Please!" Terry begged.

"Congratulations! You have been selected for the very competitive role of Man. This is the Woman. You are now allowed to mate."

The Cub Scouts lifted polaroids to their eyes. Two sat on the floor, already bored. They could not hear the Man from behind the glass.

"Hello? Please? Please! I'm not interested anymore! I want out!"

Terry banged on the door, and he suddenly felt like he had to pee. He shouted over and over again until the recording answered.

"Congratulations! You have been selected—"

"No no no! No thank you!"

"—for the very competitive role of Man. You are now allowed—"

"I don't want to, I don't want to anymore! No no!"

The recording seemed to melt and click away; when it returned it was distorted.

"Are you interested?"

"No!"

"Are you—are you interested?"

"NO! NO! NO!"

EEENNNG. The cage door shut, and the deceased chimp rolled back into the wall.

"Oh thank gosh," Terry prayed, "oh dear oh dear oh dear."

Somehow, out of everything he thought, the clearest image was how disappointed Cady would be when he came home.

"Preparing room for next session," the speaker droned.

Terry waited by the door like a cat. The door did not open. "Hello?"

Terry was feeling stupid for pleading so desperately to no one, when a deep growl of bass consumed him. It shook his bones and flexed the glass and scrambled the mulch. The pitch bent lower, lower until Terry stopped hearing it, but rather felt it rumble in his guts.

"Nn...nnn-o-o-oo-o-o-ooogGHHHH!" he shook out, as the waves beat slower then faster then slower faster in sickening pulses. His chest convulsed. The pulses tightened, growling and fighting and pounding and pulling until—

"AaauuuggGUHHH!"

Terry's lungs popped out of his mouth, followed by his stomach and three inches of bowels. He was alive long enough to taste as his guts wheezed and fizzled outside his body. He saw the flash of Polaroid cameras as he died there in the mulch.

EEENNNNGG.

Terry's body still present, the door buzzed open once more. The confident man entered, fully nude, his sex brimming with his quickening pulse.

"Congratulations! You have been selected for the very competitive role of Man."

The confident man grinned in delight.

"You're goddamn right! Hell yes. I'm gonna fuck a chim-pan-ZEE! Get me those yum yums!"

In the viewing room opposite, the Cub Scouts watched, engaged by the flesh ballet. Little Tad Taster watched most eager of all. Next year, he'd be Senior Patrol Leader.

The Story Must Be Told

THE NEW CONSCIOUSNESS IN TOWN

The 66th Story [a]

 Randy Melkin worked at the SwiftLube on Box Street for fourteen years before his consciousness dissolved, his body was subsumed, and he ceased to be a human being. After that, he worked for three more months. Randy Melkin worked at the SwiftLube on Box Street right until he laid down on its lubey floor one Thursday afternoon, closed his eyes, and stopped breathing. He was not alone when he died—far from it. In fact, Randy died with every member of the SwiftLube organism, each of them croaking instantaneously in an impressive act of synchronized dying.

 Long before Randy's mind slipped free, he was the hardest worker at the SwiftLube on Box Street. Randy owned several changes of the SwiftLube uniform—charcoal slacks and sky-blue polo shirt with his name stitched on the breast pocket—because he didn't just wear the uniform at work. He wore the outfit to

---

[a] By: Gaggles Turkeymyn.

Church every Sunday, once to a wedding, and he always wore it when picking up his daughter Amelia from soccer. He owned other clothes, but none of them swelled his eyes with dewy pride like the uniform. Really, uniform was the wrong word: the slacks and polo were vestments, an exoskeleton.

Randy's wife had died ten years prior from a hereditary condition no doctor had named, but would most fittingly be called "Dumb Lung." Her epiglottis never closed completely, and the lungs pumped saliva into themselves with every breath until she internally drowned four days after Christmas. Some men turn to drinking after such a loss, others to the Church, but when Randy found healing, it was in the lube-streaked concrete of the SwiftLube on Box Street.

First, he found calm in the routine, changing oil and spreading lubricant until the tradition of it distracted him from crying. Then he found friendship in the clients and mechanics, a network of trust and companionship to replace the love he lost. Finally, he found wisdom in the SwiftLube corporate culture. There was a certain attention to detail, purpose in the challenging quotas, and peace in repetition that filled the gaps in his heart like sealant on a gasket. In quiet moments alone with the employee handbook, Randy sensed a loving spirit between the words and diagrams, a wisdom guiding the midwestern chain from above. He was more correct than he could anticipate.

It was a late Tuesday afternoon when the dissolution occurred. Though the mechanics Randy managed had left for the day, Randy was still helping an elderly woman who had brought in her Oldsmobile Alero for a tire rotation minutes before closing.

"Are you sure it's not a bother?" the woman asked.

"You couldn't bother me if you tried!" Randy grinned over the pneumatic groan of the car lift.

He stepped under the rusted vehicle for a cursory inspection. He felt at home here, and gazing up at the undercarriage, he felt a strange peace settle into him, like bread sopping up honey. He knew what the car required, he knew how fast it would take, and how much it would cost. He knew which tools he would need, how many times he'd turn the wrench, and he knew which tire would be first and which tire would be last. It was all so certain. In that moment, his brain and habits were kindling, wet with gasoline, unknowingly eager for a spark.

Eyes to the ceiling, a single drip of oil gathered, fell, and wet the crease between Randy's brows.

Plunk.

A minute of silence passed, Randy gazing skyward, unmoving.

"Is there a problem?" the elderly woman asked.

Randy would have responded, but he no longer understood words, which oddly did not bother him. His consciousness had fallen to pieces. His free will crisped in a blaze. His train of thought stopped, the passengers exited their cars in an orderly fashion, then drowned themselves in an adjacent river. Randy was anointed. Drool began to gather on his lip, and dribbled to stain the sky-blue polo.

If before Randy had imagined his soul as a chatty little point between his ears, now he felt like it was a booming giant dot, so large it contained everything he saw. Strangely, this change didn't make it harder to function—if anything, his body suddenly made sense.

"Sir?" the woman inquired.

"Uhhhhnnnnnnggg," Randy responded.

Though he could speak no actual words, Randy completed the tire rotation with alien focus. He also changed the oil, replaced the windshield wipers, refilled the coolant, and sealed the gaskets, each in record time. Though the shapes of the numbers held no meaning to Randy, he punched the buttons of the cash register to accurately read $248.

"Uhhnnfff," Randy told the woman.

"I only had enough for the rotation," the woman replied.

With surprising speed, Randy's body raised a wrench over his head and swung at the woman, breaking the wrist she raised in defense. He swung again, but she tumbled back beyond his reach. She fled, and consumed by novel passion, Randy followed her—for just three more seconds. Then the clock struck 7. Closing time. Wrench in hand, Randy locked the doors, closed the garage, and collapsed to dreamless sleep on the concrete. The Randy that was was gone. Having shed the clumsy weight of humanity, he had become a cell for a new, more encompassing organism. Randy was now SwiftLube.

The next morning, moments after the SwiftLube on Box Street opened, the mechanics arrived to find Randy hard at work on a Chevy Nova. The driver side window was shattered apart, and though they were unaware, the license plate matched the report for a missing vehicle being filed that very instant. A mechanic in a wrinkled polo tried to make a joke.

"Huh huh, geez Randy, didya even leave last night?"

Randy said nothing in response. He merely twisted his wrench and let oil drip down his forehead in greasy sacrament.

"Jeezus, Randy, you don't need to do that, here, let me—"

Before the mechanic in the wrinkled shirt could intervene, Randy slammed his palm into the bridge of the man's nose. Blood sputtered from his nose in cherry globs, and he wailed loudly.

"Ahh! I wa jutht tryna helb!"

Randy promptly returned to the Nova to finish repairs on

the rusting undercarriage. He had already forgotten about the incident, though his palm still stung from shattering the man's nasal bone. While another coworker escorted the bloodied mechanic to the ER, Randy equalized the tires, replaced the broken window, and returned the car to where he found it. The newer hires were startled by Randy's behavior, but the veteran mechanics reassured them:

"Don't worry, he gets like this. After his wife died? Oof, he weren't shit for a conversation, but he doubled his quota that month."

In a week's time, Randy would do more than double his quota: he would meet the quotas of each and every worker in the SwiftLube on Box Street. After a few days of the new Randy, the mechanics formerly under his supervision had reversed roles, watching Randy do their work for them, disturbed and enthralled in equal parts by his newfound efficiency. It was eerie, yet undeniably impressive.

That same day, Amelia arrived at the SwiftLube on Box Street with a counselor from the school, Mrs. Gladwurst. After the girl had failed to attend school for three days with no excuse from a parent, Mrs. Gladwurst drove to the Melkin household and discovered the inconsolable student.

The day of Randy's transformation, Amelia had walked home from soccer to find an empty house. She called her father's cell phone 48 times, leaving 36 messages. She had gone into shock over fear of losing yet another parent, and, much like Randy ten years earlier, had avoided her fears with diligent, thought-suffocating work. Mrs. Gladwurst entered the sunbleached Melkin residence to find the fifteen-year-old scrubbing the oven with a toilet brush, her soccer uniform covered in soot and cleaning solution. The counselor sprang to action. She called family, the Church, the police, and Randy's bank. Finally, she called the SwiftLube on Box Street.

"Randy's not dead," said a confused voice on the phone, "he's breakin' records!"

Amelia and the counselor arrived at the SwiftLube soon after. Upon hearing their approach, Randy waved Mrs. Gladwurst's car into the garage to replace the squealing brake pads.

"Dad?" Amelia asked the man who was once her father.

Randy ignored her voice, instead pushing his only living relative and Mrs. Gladwurst out of the car and onto the garage floor. He drove the car onto a lift as the counselor attempted to shout for his attention. He stepped out, and wheeled himself beneath the vehicle.

"Dad, what's wrong?" the girl sobbed, tears forming trails through the soot on her cheeks. "Dad?"

Randy's body looked his daughter in the eye. It was a coincidence, of course—the box of brake pads was sitting on a bench behind her. All the same, Amelia saw the vacancy in Randy's eyes, the same she had seen in her mother's embalmed corpse. She remembered how devoted Randy became to his job in those following months. She remembered how his role as parent became more duty than vocation. She remembered how Randy started saying "I love you" with all the frequency and gusto of ordering a salad. She then cried, but after a few minutes of tears, she tugged on Mrs. Gladwurst's skirt.

"I'm ready to go home now."

Amelia would be the only human not surprised by her father's transformation—in a way it explained everything.

Randy's behavior, the incident with the daughter especially, had the whole staff of the SwiftLube worried. Yet, none of them tried to stop him, least of all the mechanic with the broken nose. Belvin Little, Randy's assistant manager, tried taking a less confrontational approach. He simply stood by Randy, helping him gather tools, talking to him in calm, even tones. Belvin figured eventually he would break through, find the raw nerve in Randy's brain that would explain his behavior. It was the opposite that happened.

After two days of gentle assistance, while they were repairing a leaky gasket, Belvin felt his thoughts go foggy, colorless. He would've said it was like falling asleep, that is if words still meant anything to him. One minute, it was a man and a human-sized cell working on a Honda Civic, the next minute, they were just two cells.

In nature, there are many phenomena scientists would call a "state change." The most recognizable for humans is water turning to ice. After a certain threshold of temperature and pressure, molecules of water change alignment, stack themselves, and self-organize. It takes only a single crystal of ice to spur the transition, infecting each neighboring molecule with its new rules. Randy was a similar kind of crystal, but not a crystal of physical properties, rather, a crystal of consciousness. Belvin was the second crystal, and he would not be the last.

Three days after Belvin's transformation, four other employees similarly shed their humanity. Now a team of six, the cells quickly met the SwiftLube branch's yearly quota in just a single week. Five days after that, the entire staff of the SwiftLube on Box Street was converted to cells of the SwiftLube organism. Before, Randy's means for carrying out SwiftLube's desires were limited. Now, with a whole organ's worth of devoted corporate husks, SwiftLube was capable of far grander deeds.

On the following Monday morning, the cells of the

SwiftLube on Box Street woke up exactly when the store opened for the day. They gathered wrenches in their hands, left the garage, and marched down Box Street in formation like a Roman guard. The first faulty car they encountered was a Volkswagen Rabbit. Several members of the formation now had specialized roles, and upon hearing the crackling wheeze of a broken catalytic converter, they began to chirp in guttural yelps.

"Yewyew yewyew yewyewyew!"

In cohesive movements, human appendages of the SwiftLube organism reached out to the car, ripped the door open, and forcefully ejected the driver and passenger waiting at a red light.

"What the fuck what the fuck what the—" was all the driver could disagree before being brained by a wrench to the temple. "BLEGH!" he spurted as he fell to the ground, blood pooling in his ears.

The passenger ran to the sidewalk, trying to bargain, taking off her rings and throwing her cash. She ran to the police shortly after, but if she had waited a mere twenty minutes, she would've seen the car returned to the same stop light with a brand new catalytic converter purring quietly. The blood would even be mopped.

The police weren't sure what to make of the report, but soon it was no longer a single incident. There were 68 cases of forced repairs that first day, double that many the next when the SwiftLube on Eagle Boulevard was likewise assimilated. Within a month, every SwiftLube in the state operated under a single consciousness. The reports of carnage soon overwhelmed the local police precincts, many of whom saw their own family subsumed by the toxic corporate entity.

A federal investigator was sent to the town, and drove

only four yards into the SwiftLube service area before an organ of grease-stained hands and blue polo shirts dragged him bleeding through what, seconds prior, was only a chipped windshield, now a collection of safety glass chunklets. After he woke, but before he died, he alerted the National Guard.

"Steady, hold steady," the acting commander spoke over earpiece to her soldiers. They were arranged behind the Vincelli's Pizza at the intersection of Box Street and Germain Avenue. Another battalion was across the street, surveying from an abandoned real estate office, and another was two blocks down on Dupont Road organizing medical tents, jeeps, and three tanks. It was 06:58 hours. By this point, accounts had grown from interviews on local news affiliates to recurring segments on 24-hour news networks. The most memorable clip showed mobs of blue-shirted middle-aged men carefully buckling a blood-stained infant car seat into an empty sedan. The commander had seen the carnage remotely, but it did not adequately prepare her. Sweat stung her eyes as the clock struck 07:00 hours, and blinking, she missed the moment the hordes of human cells streamed from the SwiftLube in an unholy human amoeba. She heard the gunshots first.

"Fire! Fire! Fire!"

Over the course of two and a half hours, the National Guard shot and killed forty-two cells of SwiftLube. In that same time, the Guard lost sixty-eight wholly individual men and women. Some were bludgeoned by wrenches, others ripped into meaty chunks by circles of grasping, nailless fingers. At 09:33 hours, they were ordered to retreat.

A group of high-ranking officials weighed the outcome of the massacre from the safety of an underground bunker. Drinks were provided. At first these leaders of men discussed strategy, weaponry, and civilian casualties. But eventually, over a round of Manhattans, they noted the nearly six million dollars worth of repairs provided to their jeeps, tanks, and other such armored vehicles over the course of the onslaught. It was the Utah Senator, drinking a Shirley Temple, who said that while families were grieving, if they knew how much they had saved as taxpayers, perhaps "they'd cry a little less." From that moment on, a new approach was decided, and soon news stations in the tri-state were issuing clear warnings: "Do not engage. Run and Save."

Two months later, there was not a single worker at a single SwiftLube spared from assimilation. Drivers were accustomed to checking mirrors for roving packs of sky blue polo shirts, doors kept unlocked. Parked cars were left with their windows open. There were more deaths, but negligible in the grand scheme of overall savings. Meanwhile, SwiftLube was surpassing even the wildest of quotas. All three of their competitors shuttered locations.

The cell that was Randy Melkin had changed with the addition of so many other cells. He was out of the frontlines and back to management, adapted to join other cells as a kind of corporate thyroid. From along his spinal column, his vertebrae had sprouted hollow, bony protrusions, like skeletal drinking straws. When cries of "yewyew yewyewyew" echoed down Box Street, the cell that was Randy would form a tight circle with other such adapted cells, their backs to the center, and together they would expel pale yellow liquid from the spouts in their backs. In a previous state of consciousness, Randy may have been proud of his new job, his rapid ascension up the corporate ladder—it was quite the promotion. But now the only words he had for it were "uhnng," "yuu-ooof," and hisses of sprayed saliva.

One Thursday afternoon, after three months of forced car theft and repair, every single vehicle in SwiftLube's service areas was perfectly repaired. This included cars left abandoned on the side of the road, decades-old cars rusting in junkyards now shiny and glowing, stacked in piles by broken toasters and sanitary napkins. Inhabitants of those areas had become accustomed to the scouting cells' yews, but those listening heard something else that afternoon. At a decibel nearly out of human range, groups of SwiftLube cells began to whistle with their mouths closed like boiling kettles.

In tight formation with the other members of the thyroid, the cell that was Randy began to vibrate bodily, and from the exhaust holes dotting his spine he squirted a smoking substance the color of tar that smelled like a hot mouth. Moments later, packs of cells retreated to their SwiftLube hubs across the tri-state, leaving roads and alleys suspiciously free of sky blue polo shirts. The few cells held in government containment for study struggled against their restraints, breaking ribs and femurs in violent attempts at freedom. An hour later, they would die as calmly as all the others.

After two days of silence, when the government investigated the SwiftLube locations, they found a scene that made Jonestown look amateurish and unorganized. In neat rows of twelve, lines of human cells stretched from wall to wall of each lubey garage floor, face up, eyes open, bodies still. They did not suffocate. They were not poisoned. They simply stopped living. The bodies were sorted and delivered back to their respective families, and while Amelia was notified of her father's death, she did not cry this time. She did not request a funeral.

It was difficult to blame SwiftLube for what it had done.

This is not to say people were not angry, or that answers were not sought, and legislature passed, but that the effect was insignificant. Humans, as individuals, could not judge this new, higher realm of consciousness from their low perch in the orders of organization, no more than a bee could rebel against a hive, or a carbon atom could protest a diamond. When similar state changes occurred the following summer for Lego, PrepsiCo, and the Catholic Church, most humans ceased their efforts to understand. They stopped asking "how?", and they stopped asking "why?" If coworkers gathered around the watercooler to chat in sober voices about the latest cluster of human cells, their opinions were all variations of the same concern:

"When will it happen to us?"

The Story Must Be Told

FUN BOY LIMITED PARTY TRAVEL NUMBER ONE

The 69th Story[†]

Nine colossal obelisks crashed into nine sparsely populated areas on planet Earth. Each monolith was made out of a single, city-wide and mountain-high piece of iron.

Iron is the last element a star turns into before it collapses on itself and explodes into infinity.

The obelisks planted themselves deep into the Earth, rising out of the ground like giant telephone poles. It's unclear how many thousands of people died when this event occurred. However, large cities were spared and there was minimal loss of wildlife, livestock and crops. It seemed the landing of the obelisks was intentional and careful; respectful of life.

Naturally, Earthlings panicked. Cults spun up overnight, their followers poisoned and dead by their own hands within days. The Pope considered the obelisks from space to be a message from

---

[†] From: The Tome of Tommy Two Tome. By: Dickhead Ryan.

God Himself that He did not exist, so the Pope doused the Sistine Chapel in kerosene and burned it to the ground. He died in a hail of automatic rifle fire, shot by his very own Swiss Guards.

He was denied a Christian burial.

People turned on one another, committed mass murder, beheaded the wealthy, held orgies, and burned cities to carbon. Sashi City in China's Hubei province was wiped completely off the map when a crew of twenty-six pro-democratic revolutionaries accidentally blew up the Three Gorges Dam before they could give the Chinese government their demands.

No human being was spared the insanity caused by the obelisks. No one but Egon Soterios, a United States citizen of Greek descent. He was the first human being to live on Mars, and his mission was ending shortly. Soon he'd be on his way back to Earth.

Miraculously, no nuclear missiles were launched. Several Russian, Israeli, French and American officials admitted to clicking the red button in a frenzy, some dozens of times. But each reported that there had been some unknown technical glitch that stopped the weapons from firing.

On the fifth-and-one-halfth day, the obelisks vibrated, emitting a subsonic pulse that rumbled in molars, the pits of stomachs, and testicles. The vibration cracked the foundation of every building within 500 miles. Elephants interned at the San Diego Zoo in California, United States of America, stampeded out of their enclosures and trampled their handlers. The rampage leveled the zoo's famed bird enclosure. Scores of exotic birds were freed. Penguins died of heat stroke in the California sun.

After the pulse stopped, things settled down. People breathed a collective sigh of relief. Everyone felt a little weird, but refreshed. The tremor had felt like a nice back rub.

The vibration calmed humanity. Humans, a notoriously aggressive and competitive species, relaxed. Fires were put out and field hospitals popped up in every city, suburb, town, and village.

Russia, the United States, China, and Saudi Arabia called an emergency meeting to fund global relief efforts. Each reduced their nation's wealth to a meager operating budget "just to keep the lights on," as the fellow likes to say. The meeting took twenty-eight minutes. There was no photo op. The President of the International Court of Justice in the Hague reported back, "They got along famously. It's always nice to see old friends."

When the wealthy nations offered the money to the UN, the representatives of every nation politely declined. People were helping each other out of the goodness of their hearts. Money lost meaning. Stocks plummeted overnight, but there was no panic. Banks closed up shop and offered to send checks in the mail to clear out people's accounts. No one took them up on their offer.

People shared experiences. They spoke openly and intimately, without fear of mockery. The common thread in every conversation was that no one was having any sex.

Neurologists got to work. They discovered the obelisks' vibration neutralized the part of the human brain reserved for sexual drive and sexual competition. Fertility doctors uncovered that the rumble was so intense, rattling testicles and ovaries so strongly, that people were rendered sterile. No one panicked. Humanity felt refreshed to see no one as a sexual threat, even subconsciously.

With the drive to reproduce at any cost negated, people decided to make life better for those around them. There was a great diaspora. Humans from historically wealthy nations left for communities who needed help.

Lockheed Martin, the titan of weapons manufacturing, cleared out its plants and put their scientists to work on research and production of sustainable food.

NASA used all its people power to do all they could to end global warming. The scientists knew humanity would die out from infertility in the next 100 years, but they wanted to try to make the planet nice for all the wildlife they would leave behind.

The vibration had spared animals, who were reproducing wildly. Animals that once faced extinction roamed free from poachers.

NASA was so committed to its new mission that it forgot Egon Sotrios was out there in space, wrapping up a geological survey of the surface of Mars. He'd attempted to contact mission control for weeks but to no avail. Egon figured there had been a massive communications glitch. The A.I. in his spaceship was well-equipped to land back on Earth without the assistance of mission control. But he was nervous all the same.

Egon would be spared.

He would come to wish he hadn't been.

* * *

While humanity was hard at work to leave the planet in better shape than they'd found it, one more trick from the obelisks awaited them.

Seventeen months after landing on earth and buzzing humanity into peace, a sustained, pneumatic *fffsssshhhhhhhh* blasted out of the top of the obelisks. They shot tiny particles into the atmosphere, giving the sky a beautiful, shimmering, pinkish-purplish tint. Small flecks that looked like pollen gently rained down on Earth. The event was like a beautiful snowstorm. Humanity celebrated, grateful for yet another gift from the obelisks that had already done so much for them. People didn't know their path to extinction had accelerated.

The beautiful dust blanketed earth. It bent tree branches with its weight, gave bodies of water a stunning sheen, and sparkled in the grass like frost. Scientists took samples of the powder to their labs and began studying its properties. Within a few days, the extraterrestrial pollen sank deep into the soil and dissolved in ponds, lakes, rivers and oceans. Flecks that were caught in the sunlight, on tree branches, asphalt and concrete, vaporized into a purple fog that slowly rose to the atmosphere. Virtually all visible traces of it disappeared.

Scientists at the Center for Disease Control in Atlanta, Georgia, United States of America, studied the dust. Some theorized it was packed with micro-nutrients that would re-fertilize the soil, perhaps eliminating the plastics humanity had so carelessly poisoned the planet with. Botanists wondered if they were alien seeds that would re-forest the brutally ravaged rainforests. Global warming experts hoped the flecks were alien nanomachines, blasted into the atmosphere to reverse the effects of human-made climate change.

On Monday, the nine obelisks whirred soundlessly. The ground gently shook as they rose out of the Earth and back into the sky, floating towards space at an estimated speed of eighty-six miles per hour. In eight months and seventeen days, Egon Soterios, fast asleep in stasis, would pass them at a speed of 36,000 miles per hour.

For forty-eight hours, the world mourned the loss of the benevolent obelisks.

The following Wednesday, Dr. Kimberly Chen at the Center for Disease Control in Atlanta, Georgia, United States of America, gave a televised address to present their findings. Her face was a sickly gray. She had giant bags under her eyes and her hair was frizzy. She jiggled the microphone stand for quite some time, until it was precisely in a position that met her specifications. She cleared her throat and spoke in a froggy voice.

The atomic properties of individual flecks of pollen were indecipherable. They were composed of what looked like genetic material that seemingly bent the rules of physics and biology. On their own, they were harmless and had a short lifespan. But when combined, a reaction occurred.

A terrible one.

In the lab, the dust particles had been painstakingly separated by highly efficient robots, and stored individually in test tubes. When separated, they dehydrated, and turned to ash. 99% of the collected dust was lost. However, one clump of particles was put in a ceramic bowl in a locked room and heated under a lamp.

When the cells—for lack of a better word—touched one another under the heat, they fused. They generated their own energy and pulled more cells towards them until they were a red-hot, glowing sphere. More and more of the cosmic dust particles were sucked towards the center, until the mass began to take the shape of a human fetus, suspended in a sack of goo. The fetus in the lab came to term in two hours and forty-nine minutes, bursting out of its sack. It had the appearance of an incredibly muscular, two-foot tall, full-grown, translucent human male.

He was not cute.

He did not have the "new baby" smell.

He was grotesque, and he proved to be violent.

Lauren Kwezlowski, an intern at the CDC, went through the airlock of the sealed room to check on the tiny man. He motioned for her to come over, batting his black eyes. Terrified, she approached him with her hands up. The tiny man purred like a cat. She had a cat at home named Brandon, and the purring put her at ease. She reached out to pick the tiny man up. He raised his arms like a toddler as she brought him to her chest.

The scientists looked on in horror as the tiny man bit her throat with his flat teeth, similar to the teeth of a hippopotamus. He pulled out a chunk of her larynx and backflipped off her, gracefully landing on his tiny, clear feet. Lauren staggered backwards, eyes open, gripping her throat as life pumped out of her. The tiny man ran at her at an incredible velocity, and began eating her whole.

Emergency procedure was enacted. Machines manipulated the air pressure in the room, causing the tiny man to become dizzy. He fell asleep at Lauren's lap not unlike her cat, Brandon, now ownerless. Armed guards sealed the tiny man in a small, reinforced, explosion-proof cube.

Dr. Chen motioned from the podium for her colleagues to bring out that very cube.

The cameras at the press conference focused on the alien in the box. He sat in the lotus position, smiling gently, completely non-threatening. Some people in the audience cooed at him. Others felt like they were on the brink of evacuating their bowels out of fear.

This, Dr. Chen explained, is the violent end of humanity. Upon finishing her sentence, she pulled a pair of scissors out of her lab coat, and jammed them into her chest. She pulled them out quickly, emitting a 13-foot arterial spurt.

The press stampeded out of the room, screaming.

The public address was televised and translated across the world. One million Chinese citizens had gathered in Tiananmen Square to watch the address on a massive screen that blasted her translated words through gigantic loudspeakers. They stared in silent terror as hordes of tiny, translucent men pulled themselves out of the ground around them.

Zhang Wei Li, a former soldier-turned-florist, broke the silence with a scream. A tiny man had crawled up his back and bit into the back of his skull. He devoured Zhang quickly, bones and all, like a log in a hyperactive wood chipper. Terrified Chinese citizens charged out in every direction. They soon found they were surrounded by thousands of the tiny men, who had encircled them as they watched the address. The tiny men descended upon them and ate well. As they packed more and more human beings into their alien digestive systems, they continued to grow. The tallest of the tiny men grew to be 32 feet and 3 inches tall. Most others averaged out at 29 feet.

The extinction of humanity by the once-tiny, now-gigantic translucent men only took eight months and seventeen days. They fed only on humans. All other types of wildlife were spared, and they seemed to have no appetite for vegetables or water.

They worked very well together, and showed gruesome creativity. Some would trap humans and bat them around like cats before devouring them. Others competed to see how far they could throw a person, taking bets in alien currency.

It seemed like they were doing this for fun.

The gigantic men were immune to human weapons. They had thick skin like rhinoceri. Bullets bounced off them like raindrops on the windshield of a 1994 champagne Ford Taurus.

Humans only had small arms to defend themselves, as the vibration had incapacitated heavy, advanced weapons that relied on computerized triggers, hence the nuclear missiles not firing when this whole affair began. The alien men had taken some extreme measures, measures that one could consider not very sporting.

A pack of nine alien men corralled a crowd of thousands of English citizens and chased them off the White Cliffs of Dover. The humans burst on the rocks like tomatoes. Alien men looking for more of a challenge climbed skyscrapers in Chicago, Illinois, United States, pulling humans out and tossing them over their shoulders into the hungry mouths of titanic aliens below. A battalion of gigantic men split up and raided rainforests to suss out the last remaining humans who had fled for cover.

Alien technology scanned the Earth and found there were only seven human beings left. They had escaped to the Gobi desert.

The aliens made short work of them.

When the last confirmed human being had been killed, the "hunt" was called to an end. The gigantic aliens celebrated in an odd way, stepping to the right and left with their hands in the air, like crabs, intermittently barking in rapture. Once the bizarre festivities ended, all the gigantic men around the world headed to Houston, Texas, United States of America, for a final ceremony. It took nineteen days for all of them to converge.

* * *

Egon Soterios' spaceship slowly woke him from months of stasis. He was forty-five minutes away from reentering the Earth's atmosphere. He stretched and yawned. He scratched himself. He felt refreshed and rested for the first time since he left his home planet.

Egon exited his hyperbaric chamber and headed for the controls of his spaceship. He flipped on his communications device to report to NASA Ground Control in Houston, Texas, United States of America. They didn't respond. He was shocked they hadn't fixed their comms system in the time it took for him to fly back to Earth. But the A.I. in his spaceship was so reliable that he figured it wouldn't have been worth the cost to get it back up and running. He frowned at the very real possibility that it was a budget issue. The United States Congress was always trying to screw the little guy.

Simultaneously, particles of business tycoon Ramis Plimmn from the planet Üt sped through space. He was scheduled to fuse and materialize in Houston, Texas, United States, mere minutes after Egon Soterios was to take his first step back on planet Earth.

Egon landed without a hitch. His ship came to a peaceful halt, and the intercom on his ship thanked him for his stay in a soothing male voice. The blast screens went down on his windows and he looked out on his home planet.

There were no American flags. There were no "WELCOME HOME, EGON!" banners. There were no mechanics on the runway, spraying his spaceship with cooling foam. But there were hundreds of thousands of gigantic, translucent men waiting to greet him.

This had to be a trick of his mind, he thought. He had to be hallucinating. He pressed a green button on a control panel to lower the exit ramp. Egon took a step, tripped, and rolled out of the ship, right at the feet of the recently-rematerialized Ramis Plimmn from the planet Üt.

"Greetings," Plimmn said in an deep, bone rattling voice.

Egon screamed as Plimmn lifted him into the air and presented him to the crowd of his alien brothers. They cheered. Some wept. Egon slithered in Plimmn's hands like a tadpole, desperate to escape. He could not.

Once the cheering died down, Plimmn set Egon on his shoulder. Egon, terrified he would fall, gripped the shoulder tightly and made no attempt to escape.

"My name is Ramis Plimmn from the planet Üt. I am the founder and CEO of a corporation that roughly translates into human English as 'Fun Boy Limited Party Travel Number One.' Üt is very far from here. The men gathered in front of you are our very top tier VIP customers. And—"

He couldn't finish his sentence over the cheers of the crowd, the men happy to make known that they had bought the most exclusive, most expensive package.

"—And they are part of the great community of Ütarians," he continued, "who get a rush from what human beings would call on their planet 'Extreme Sports.' I first got the idea when a TV signal from your planet jumbled ESPN's X-Games with a show where men hunted animals for sport. *Bingo,* I thought."

Egon vomited down his space suit. The crowd laughed politely.

"This is going to hurt your feelings," Plimmn said solemnly, "but all humanity has been ... eaten ... by these brave, action-seeking, VIP-pass holding Ütarians in front of you."

Another cheer erupted. Egon screamed.

"You are indeed honored, for you will be known in the books of Ütarian history as the last man to die on planet Earth."

Egon rose to his feet, scrambling to jump off the shoulder of the towering man. Plimmn held him in place as a shorter, older looking alien approached them, holding a silver bowl with small rectangles in it. They looked like dominos.

Plimmn reached into the bowl, mixed them around, and pulled out one of the rectangles. "The winner is," he announced in his alien tongue, "Krenn Bnorn of West Üt!"

"That's me!" an immense, translucent man shouted from the back.

"Make way!" yelled Plimmn. Although the other men were disappointed, they cheered for Krenn all the same. Krenn made his way through the crowd to Plimmn, and they hugged. He was given a certificate to a family-style eatery back on Üt, not unlike the American chain restaurant "Applebee's."

"Do you have any words for us?" asked Plimmn.

"Um," stammered Krenn. He was no public speaker. "Thanks for the memories, Mr. Plimmn. And, um, it was a ton of fun and um, I can't wait to go back to my family and tell them all about it."

The crowd roared triumphantly.

"Very well put," said Plimmn. "Enjoy the grand prize!"

Plimmn lifted Egon and set him in the massive hands of Krenn. Egon screamed and attempted to escape, but this would prove impossible. Krenn raised Egon to the crowd. They roared. Krenn theatrically lifted Egon into the air, clasped between his thumb and finger, and dropped him into his gigantic mouth. He chewed savagely, grinding Egon to mush.

Krenn swallowed and bowed.

The audience went wild.

Eventually, the commotion died down.

It was time to go home.

The men traded their contact information and clapped each other on the back as they waited to disintegrate back into pollen and get scooped up by the obelisks, then sent back to Üt.

They would remember it as the best trip of their lives, and they all agreed the VIP package was worth it.

The Story Must Be Told

THEY MADE A STRANGE LOVE

The 60th Story ⚘

"There is no space for you," the host whispered to the couple. "I must ask you to leave." He would not look them in the eye.

The man wanted to argue—he could see empty tables. They weren't even going to sit, just discreetly order a slice with the change they gathered. But he knew it was not a matter of space. His partner tugged at his sleeve—*let's go*. They were both used to this, but she attracted a different degree of hostility.

"Sure, sure," the man scowled.

Hidden under the sound of patrons sucking straws, scattered fragments of "wanna try mine?", "how was work?", and the low hum of top 40s hits, two bellies groaned.

When the woman walked, she faltered like a newborn deer, so the man supported her wherever they went. Tonight, as usual, they ambled down Gates Avenue. Their four legs together

---

⚘ From: The Book of Cro Croa Honest. By: Winifresh Puristink.

could equal one slow person. They never made it to the shelter before it closed. She wasn't treated well there either. It didn't matter how cold it got—the man preferred a night in the open if it meant she was safe, if they could spend it with each other. Don't get any ideas, though.

In their two months together, the man had never seen the woman without her coat. If he really thought about it, he wasn't sure she was a she—the way he identified people did not apply to her. Her face was bandaged to hide all but one eye, obscured even then by weeds of patchy hair. Her hands were large, but her feet were tiny. Her odor was not masculine or feminine, but milky. That said, she liked when he called her his gal, or with a laugh, his lady. As far as he figured, that settled it. The man did not look traditional himself, overlarge, lumbering, scarred by neglect and hard years. They didn't discuss the past. There were questions you did not ask.

They heard feet running up the sidewalk.

"Out of the way!" a teenage boy shouted.

Two boys barreled through, the last one colliding with the man. The man lost his grip, and the woman fell onto the sidewalk with a pained cry like a voiceless kitten. She was fragile.

One kid, chin and neck patchy with proud hairs, caught a look of the woman and heaved.

"What the fuck is that?" he asked. The boys elbowed each other and laughed.

The man clenched his jaw; a tooth cracked. He did not like when anger took him over, but sometimes it was warranted. He lost himself then to a creature that knew what to do with the inherent violence in his size. He ran to the boy and shoved him to the ground. He picked the kid up by his jacket, blood pounding in his ears, when he heard his companion. The words were whispered but unmissable.

"I'm ok."

Then the anger was gone. He had torn the boy's puffy jacket. He let it go. Bending down, the man gathered the woman. The boy's friend had backed away, hands up in surrender while the boy groaned on the sidewalk. They looked like they were fifteen. The couple shuffled away.

"I'm sorry," the man said.

"You don't have to be," the woman smiled.

The way a smile lifted her voice, the way it rounded her syllables like a chime, the way he knew she smiled even with his eyes closed, lit the man up inside. He never thought he would know intimacy. In the rare quiet of the evening city, gratitude overwhelmed him.

It was on Gates Avenue when they saw the thing that made the man stop. The woman had never seen anything like it, though she could recognize the components: a chair, tires, little roller wheels, handles. It was abandoned in the mouth of an alley, plastic bags and broken glass its only companions.

The man waited a full ten minutes across the street for the owner to emerge. He would not abide stealing a thing like this—that's as bad as horse theft, he figured, if you were back in the day. But *discovering* it was a different matter.

Finally, the man decided to give it a look. He thought a wheel must be busted, the frame rusted through. But as he approached, it held up under scrutiny. At a touch, it rolled with ease. He hurrahed and slapped his knee with the back of his hand.

"What is it?" The woman asked.

"What is it?" The man laughed.

"What is it?" She was embarrassed now.

He laughed harder. "Honey, it's a wheelchair! You never seen a wheelchair?"

She wouldn't meet his eyes. The woman hated being teased, especially about her seemingly perpetual confusion. He laughed at her stubbornness, and walked her to the chair. Gently, the man lowered her inside.

"*This*, my dear, is a wheelchair."

"But what is it?"

"It's our ticket to warm beds and hot meals, that's what it is. Get a load of this!"

He pushed on the handles, and the chair began to pick up speed. The woman gripped the armrests, objecting loudly. The man heard the smile on her face. He ran faster, and tipped the chair back so her feet were in the air. She squealed not a human squeal, but a strange high frequency click. He joined her with a wail of his own, and apartments ten blocks away could hear the couple in their strange delight, a wheelchair hitting 12 miles per hour down a hill.

Never seen a wheelchair? The man pondered his new companion, this woman he knew nothing about, this woman not a woman. He wondered what it was exactly he had fallen in love with.

By the time they reached the overpass, the woman was worn out from laughing, a new kind of exhaustion for her. Though it had grown cold with each longer night, the man kept their hovel under the Box Street overpass warm. He found itchy pink insulation at a construction site, wrapped it in duct tape and bags till it was safe to sleep on. Add this to the salvaged children's sleeping bag and a final wrap of plastic bags, and they could survive most nights.

Tonight though, was colder than usual. What had been bearable in the day, under brisk night, was debilitating. The man gathered all the layers he could, and they huddled together. Still the cold found them. He held his arms around the woman, but through her coat, through his, he felt no warmth.

"We ain't gonna stay warm like this," the man sighed.

The woman's mouth chattered, but teeth did not clack.

"We need body heat, both bodies."

"Ok."

She did not understand.

"I mean we gotta undress. Skin to skin, so's we can warm each other."

The woman did not say anything for a long while. He was about to apologize, when she began to unzip her coat. He blinked his eyes, frozen. He too began to undress.

They were together under the child's sleeping bag in seconds. The woman warmed little at first. Then he draped his arm around her, and she felt his heat, a living hairy furnace. The cold pressed them together.

The man, if he was being honest, had imagined what this might be like. Though nothing about the woman was traditional, he wanted her in the normal ways—but so much more than that. He wanted to listen to her breathing. He wanted to cook her breakfast. He wanted to fall asleep with his head in her lap, her hand in his thin hair. But mixed in with it all, he wanted to see the woman he had come to love.

The coat was gone. Though he could not see her body in the dark, he could feel her. Touch painted a strange picture. She was warm, but oddly ... pliable. Under his hand, the flesh sunk like a memory foam mattress, gripping his hand gently.

"You were right," she sighed with a smile he did not have

to see, "this is warmer."

The back of the woman was like warm putty, molding to his shape. He felt a shiver quake up through a spine that wasn't there—she was ridgeless, like a water balloon.

He wanted to ask one of those questions he knew you don't ask. But, when she began to sob quietly, she asked him one first.

"Why do you do all this?"

Unexpected as her flesh was, he cradled her closer. "Why do I do all this?"

"Helping me. When I walk. Finding food. You're risking yourself. You're cold, and hungry. There's no advantage for you. So why?"

"Why? I ... I want to. Don't know why."

She shook in his arms, and sobbed harder. "Then you're sick. There's something wrong in your mind."

The man laughed.

"Heh, well, if you put it like that." He inhaled her, that warm dairy smell. "It is a sickness, I suppose. But it's a good sickness."

The woman breathed deep, made a soft clicking noise, and went calm in his arms.

"A good sickness," he repeated. "That's what love is." He hesitated. "I love you."

"Ok," she said. "... And what's that?"

The man did not laugh at her confusion this time. He did not repeat her question. He turned silent. Then he began to cry.

The woman was ashamed at once. She retracted from him, curled in on herself, sure she had offended him somehow. She felt the cold at once.

"I don't mean to be confused. This is a confusing place."

"No," he sniffled. "It ain't that. It's just—that's the gosh darn saddest thing I ever heard."

The man, she realized, was not upset, not with her anyhow. He brought her back into his warmth. They turned to one another, and he saw her body. She was not a woman, and not a man either, nor entirely human. Her flesh rippled like living ocean, a strange fluid in human shape, but frozen, blocky, cracked and worn. She was a fluid that had aged and endured. Yet her face was still hidden under its wrappings.

"So, what is it? Love?"

"I don't think I can explain it."

He pulled her closer. Gazing into her one visible eye, he saw colors he did not know in nature. The iris teemed, pulsed, and floresced. Large as he was, he felt very small.

He began to unwrap the bandages.

"But maybe I can show you."

Piece by piece, he removed the wrapping, until he saw her face. The hair had been false—it fell away with the bandages. She was smooth, rippling, and bright. She had but the one eye. The rest of her face was scattered and uncanny, an impressionist version of what a face might be. It was constructed to the best of her ability—a nose not quite centered, a mouth too large. The ears and teeth and hair were ignored for the features she knew best, like a kid learning to draw. She was an artist's interpretation of a human, he thought of his love. The pair kissed, and warmth found them at last.

The flesh that had been malleable in the cold, putty in confusion, was dextrous and sensuous in love. As their mouths moved within each other, the flesh spread like a slow motion wave crashing. She folded around him, plied him, stirred about and inside him. Pieces of her wrapped his arms like ribbon, and wherever it allowed, their passion made a union of the two. Her fluid cradled the webs of his fingers and the notches of his spine. The couple made a strange love, and stirred warm with electric hum through the long cold night.

When the woman woke, the sun was rising, the cold not quite as cold. She noticed what had been taken, but did not tell the man.

"Good morning," he cooed into her ear.

Her face absorbed into the front of her head and reformed out the back to greet him. He laughed at the trick—he would need to get used to it.

"Good morning to you," she said, and they pressed their foreheads together.

"I hope that was alright," the man grinned, "I ain't ever done it like that, but, well, I figure we can try again if it weren't ok."

"It was just right," she smiled, and instead of seeing the smile, he felt it, under his own mouth. Then his eyes went wide.

"The wheelchair!"

He was up, naked as he was, running about in sudden alarm. The chair was nowhere to be seen. He slapped his thigh, fell to his hams, and pouted. The woman draped the sleeping bag about her mystery flesh, and tried to comfort him.

"It's ok, it's ok," she whispered, but he would not calm.

"You don't take a wheelchair!" He despaired. "That's like taking a man's horse!"

The woman could make no sense of this, but did not press him.

"This species!" He cried. "This whole goddamn planet! It's all broken."

That one eye turned to him then. Whatever fury burned

inside, he felt grateful again.

"Every species is broken," she said, rubbing her facsimile hand through his hair. "But yours can break into something good."

"Not all the time," he grumbled.

"But sometimes."

She took his hand, and brought it to her chest. It sank into the wrist, and within, he felt a strange organ pump in calm rhythm.

He could not help the question then.

"Where are you from?"

She sighed, released his hand. "That doesn't matter now."

He walked weakly, wobbled in each step. This time, she took his arm, and pulled him into her. Her flesh gave, absorbed first his hand, then his forearm, then the shoulder like a limbless, plush hug. His body within her, he no longer felt nude, clothed as he was in his love. She was the warmth of last night, resolute against the chill of morning. His tired left leg joined with hers, and he felt both his foot tingling in her sentient liquid, and her foot cool on the pavement. Their faces pressed together, cheek to cheek. He closed his eyes, and for a moment saw the city through her eye—bright, foreign, and wondrous.

The man laughed, and she laughed with him. He realized how alone he felt inside just one body. He realized how empty all bodies are. Their four legs made one slow person. Alone, together, they walked down Gates Avenue.

The Story Must Be Told

The Story Must Be Told

Seasons of the Story

Revelation

The Story Must Be Told

THE STORY OF REVELATION: THE REVELATION OF STORY

The New Story ⚜

CHAPTER 1: THE RELIGION THAT WAS REAL

Far as I reckon, you could start this one here just 'bout anywhere—
—the chimp enclosure at the Cincinnati Zoo, Jax's basement next to a poster for *The Departed*, a vomit-adjacent chalkboard in San Juan, or in gosh darn heaven itself—
—but I'm starting it here:
Two girls sat crisscross applesauce in an Indiana bedroom.
—and here:
In a government office, Tony, Tiff, and Jax reviewed the terms for tax exemption in IRC Section 501(3)(c).
Trisha, the older of the two girls, checked side to side for witnesses. She licked her remaining baby teeth.

⚜ From: this book, you goof. By: the Clergy.

"I dare you to take the Lord's name in vain."

Meanwhile, Tony, Tiff, and Jax signed their initials, armpits damp with sweat, giving each other giddy little glances—*it's happening!*

"I don't know, Trisha," said Becksha, who was eight years old, mind you. "Pastor Gary says that's as bad as the F-word."

"Then you can't sleep over."

"No!"

"That's the rules," Trisha told her square.

"But I have my sleeping bag!"

"Doesn't matter. I'll call your mom."

This put Becksha in a thick pickle.

"Okay, just once."

Federal clerk Amelia Bodducelli reviewed the documents, verified the signatures were in the right place. Jax waited for some error to arise. It couldn't be this easy.

"You're all set," Amelia said.

She stamped form after form. Tony, Tiff, and Jax elated at each *thump*. Over six long months, they had loved this dream like a child. A dream born of their own hearts and minds—conceived around a lunch table in the seminary cafeteria, matured in Jax's basement, nurtured until it could meet the legal minimum requirements. After such effort and struggle, this dream was finally real: a version of Methodism that allowed communion wine. But not just wine: communion beer, communion whiskey shooterz, communion margaritas, all of it. With the final stamp, it was a real, 100% tax-exempt religion.

"Congratulations."

At that exact moment, in the Indiana bedroom, Becksha swallowed her spit, closed her eyes, and blurted:

"God dammit!"

Fire consumed her in a flash so intense it sucked the air from Trisha's lungs. Her screams echoed through every inch of the house, even the patio. The fire ripped a portal through the floor. Underneath was not the family room, but a brimstone-reeking ether of howls and demonsong. It took only seconds—the child fell body and soul within.

Trisha backed against the wall, fighting to regain her breath as her eight-year-old neighbor disappeared.

"Oh my God!"

In response, fire consumed her, and the floor opened again in its unnatural way.

The two girls were just beginning their torment of a million-million years as Tony, Tiff, and Jax ate loaded cheese poppers at Buffalo Wild Wings.

For some folks, sure, the events that followed must've been mighty affirming, worth celebrating. But remember this:

For every smug believer, there were two little girls in hell.

A lot happened during those first few minutes. In a flash of fire so bright it could be seen from space, 230 million men and 180 million women met the same end for their crime: masturbation. The extreme heat and concentration of sin burned Las Vegas, Amsterdam, and Toledo to instant ashes, leaving only fallout shadows of gambling, fornication, and for Toledo: bestiality. What folks came to call the "Erutpar," swallowed some 522,000,000 sinners. Only one man on planet Earth knew why.

In San Juan, Puerto Rico, next to his toilet, 62-year-old physics professor Israel "Izzy" Manuel finally cracked the prize gem of physics: the unified theory. He was coming down from food poisoning, and the mixture of vomit in his nose and half-digested clams in the toilet kicked his brain into a new realm. He was groaning into the porcelain when he thought:

"What if you carry the 1?"

He crawled to his chalkboard, and did just that. With this change, the whole formula exploded. Variables switched sides, factors canceled out, gravity became magnetism and electricity gravity. The string of mathematical symbols took on new logic, and the realization stunned Izzy onto his bottom. The theory was more than a simple equation unifying the forces of the universe. It was a revelation.

"The 10,000th ... the 10,000th—oh NO!"

Izzy called the governor, demanding a Zoom call with the President of the United States.

The President, that very minute, was being briefed on the sudden disappearance of one third of his electorate. Central Intelligence was blaming Russia, while the FDA believed it was peanut butter. An aide put the President on a Zoom call with a man speaking rapid fire Spanglish.

"Slow down!" said the President. "Tell it to me straight, doc."

"The unified theory is not an equation at all. It is a message written into the very fabric of the universe! It explains everything we've just seen!"

"Suppose I believe you: what does it say?"

"Follow the math." Izzy wrote the equation on a piece of paper and held it to the screen. "Watch how it changes when I carry the 1."

The President, a Mormon, watched how the message materialized from the math, akin to writing 58008 on a calculator and flipping it upside down.

"No, it—it can't be!"

"But it is," Izzy declared. "The math says it all: Whatever's the 10,000th religion … is true!"

The President's jaw fell slack.

"True? What do you mean, 'true?' Not truer than Mormonism!"

Izzy wiped his face with his hands.

"What do you think it means? Their religion is the one true religion! Their god is our God! Their rules are the rules of the universe! Every equation, every concept, every soul *is theirs to decide*."

"Are you telling me, if these jokesters say the world is flat … it is?"

"Sir, if what I told you is true, a flat world is the least of our concerns. We're talking the fate of every American—and the universe to boot!"

The President's forehead beaded with sweat. He waved an intern over, and whispered in her ear. He finally looked as scared as Izzy knew he ought to.

"Stay exactly where you are—we're sending a helicopter."

Tony, Tiff, and Jax finished their meal at Buffalo Wild Wings. They thought it was just a kitchen mishap when screams and fire erupted from the kitchen. Jax was more upset he never received his loaded potato skins, so instead of a tip, on the check he wrote "Jesus Christ is the way the truth and the light." The waiter was astounded to find it glowing with ethereal light as the clergy left for their Hyundai Sonatas.

The trio drove to the abandoned Dairy Queen where their Church was set to be constructed. They didn't notice all the cars smoldering on the side of the road, empty. Behind the cash register at DQ, they shared a celebratory round of whiskey shooterz from Tony's flask. Tiff was confident what they had taken to calling

"Crystal Methodism" would attract a hip crowd of Christians eager for bold, flavorful sacraments. She had no idea how right she was. Chanting rang out from the streets.

"Save us! Save us! Save us!"

Tony went to the drive thru window, and like Izzy earlier, was stunned onto his bottom. This is what he saw: a hundred thousand people blistering with sores, weeping, climbing over fences, splashing through gutters, mounting cars, singing hymns. Each followed the dazzling light of a new star, which went supernova 240 million years ago. It eradicated an entire solar system of planets and unique alien life, all so it could, eons later, declare an abandoned Dairy Queen the new Mecca.

Tiff checked her phone after a confusing text from her mother—*r u on fire? Pls tell me ur saf!!!* Mama Tiff had just seen the headline on CNN: "Millions Consumed in Hellfire! CDC Issues Moratorium on Blasphemy, Self-Love."

Jax, meanwhile, as the official head of Crystal Methodism LLC, heard none of the chanting. He could not even see. He fell to his knees, head ringing with celestial dial tone, palms raised skyward. On the other end of a telepathic line, the unwholesome cacophony of a celestial body squirmed into fresh life, a sound no human should be able to withstand. Blood vessels sizzled in Jax's brain, his body heated to 108 degrees Fahrenheit, yet he survived! As his temperature climbed, a gnarled voice congealed inside his brain, a voice he swore he heard his whole life but now heard honest, the words rattling bones in his chest:

"Hey Jax, it's, um. It's God."

God couldn't remember anything before that fateful day of May 22. No birth, no time eternal, just a blank void. The God of the Crystal Methodists didn't exist before Tony, Tiff, and Jax asked him to. Maybe there was another god before. I dunno. But after May 22? No ma'am—no god 'cept God.

This God did not make humans. Humans made him, a product of vindication fantasies and puzzle answers, and thus: a pained, malformed thing. He was not unlike a celestial, omniscient pug. And he knew it. God did not choose this grotesque existence, and though all powerful, he could not direct this power by his own whims. It was kind of a genie scenario.

Moments after birth, God began to work. He spent hours studying the inconsistencies in Tony, Tiff, and Jax's LLC agreement.

"This makes no fuckin' sense."

He groaned while perusing their dogma, scribbled in a spiral-bound notebook. He saw the promises of eternal damnation for sexual self pleasure.

"What the shit."

He saw the rules on taking his name in vain.

"Oh, come on."

But he couldn't say no. He closed his eyes, wiggled his ears, and thus sent the unfortunate millions to hell. Minutes into existence, his hands were awful bloody.

"What next do you ask of your God?" He spoke into Jax's brain. Jax just slapped his ears with his palms, head spinning.

"What is going on?!" Jax demanded.

So God told him the whole deal.

"You know those radio contests, where whoever's the 10th caller wins tickets to see Fuel? Or when a Radio Shack gives its 1000th customer a bunch of batteries? Well, there's one written into the universe, and it's this: whatever's the 10,000th religion … is *true*. Congratulations, bud."

Jax absorbed the news as Tony and Tiff welcomed their

new congregants. Tiff laid her hands on faces, and saw their bursting sores healed by touch. Tony shook his head and laughed.

"We're gonna need a bigger Dairy Queen!"

The President survived only three hours before hellfire consumed him for excessive Mormonism. The Vice President served as President for just ten minutes before a "Jesus Fucking Christ" cast him below. When Professor Izzy met the President, she had been, minutes prior, the Secretary of the Interior.

"Tell it to me straight, doc," she told the professor, unaware the previous President had said the same thing.

"On the helicopter over, I finally reached the IRS. We pinpointed the 10,000th religion. It was approved yesterday at 5:22 p.m.—"

"When the fires broke out!"

Izzy nodded solemn.

"So ... so what is it?"

Izzy's voice went low, as though speaking the name of a ghost.

"Madam President, it's ... Crystal Methodism."

Her hand flew over her mouth.

"Oh my God."

Flames flashed, the floor gasped open, and she was gone. Izzy didn't flinch.

Personnel escorted the next President into the room.

"Tell it to me straight, doc."

An hour later, out of options, the Oval Office support staff swore Izzy in as President. Being the grandson of a strict Catholic, he knew how to respect the name of the Lord. He made an immediate announcement over every major network.

"There's a new religion in town, everyone. And it's not like the other ones. This one is TRUE. You can trust me: I'm a scientist. The United States, to save its people, is declaring a national religion. We encourage every nation to do the same. As of this moment, under penalty of law, we are all *Crystal Methodists*."

That hour, the fires in America stopped. Well, not completely, but they became tolerable. While it wasn't the most constitutional of laws, the immediate results swayed people. In the end, Crystal Methodism wasn't *that* different from mainstream Christianity. Plus it had mimosas.

There was an official swearing-in ceremony in Washington. Tony, Tiff, and Jax all wore their nicest pants. They met the President on a platform erected under the Washington Monument, which now smoldered at a more humble 15 feet.

"Thank you, Tony, Tiff, and Jax, for not just being the one true religion, but. Well, you know. For also being American. It is good to be on the, on the uh, the right side of things."

President Izzy couldn't figure out how to end his speech. He was still new to this President thing. In a flash, something came to him.

"So, in conclusion, the Story of Crystal Methodism is the Story of America, and the Story ... The Story Must Be Told."

Everyone clapped. Tony teared up, Tiff gleamed, but Jax couldn't focus. Inside his brain, God was swearing.

"Fuck fuck fuck what the fuck."

God had been changing the trash can when his God sense tingled. All at once, he saw what was happening in Washington. He tore the trash bag open in a sudden fit. Trash juice splashed all over the floor. God burst into tears. He tugged at the golden bracelets on his wrist—more like shackles.

"There goes the universe."

After the swearing in, other countries followed the example of the United States, and soon every human with a nationality was a Crystal Methodist. Other religions didn't like this, no ma'am. The Pope delivered a scathing webcast.

"Crystal Methodism is FALSE. The founders of this-a heresy will a-burn in hell!"

Thousands of former Catholics in e-attendance witnessed sores and lesions blossom on the Pope's face like furious acne. He collapsed in a fit, grinding his teeth and biting his tongue to coleslaw.

A council of imams in Istanbul, Turkey rejected the claim from America of a new one true religion.

"This is bullshit!" they all said, more or less. Each man in attendance went both mute and, as tests would later reveal, sterile.

All the gold in Vatican City turned to plastic. The Bhagavad Gita turned to ash. All the fruit juice in Methodist fridges turned to wine. For the Crystal Methodists, it was a heady thrill.

Their first official service in the renovated Dairy Queen broke every fire ordinance in the city. Tiff healed leprosy and lupus, Tony poured shots and suds as the blood of Christ, and Jax spoke in tongues that all who listened could understand. They cleared over 800K in donations. Counting the cash and traveler's checks in the rectory was the happiest any of them had ever been.

CHAPTER 2: THE PROBLEM OF HELL

In hell, Trisha and Becksha were growing bored. Though only a month had gone by on Earth, in helltime over two hundred years had passed. The little girls who had entered hell at so tender an age had spent twenty times as long learning the ins and outs of damnation. They were becoming experts.

"Had my tongue-flogging yesterday. Ended with the Deft-Hand Swirl."

"Typical."

"The torture I can stand. It's the lack of imagination that kills me."

After a few lifetimes of torture, all pain was dull. There was nothing hell could do, no torture so terrifying, that with enough time wouldn't become tedious. Slowly, Trisha and Becksha began skipping their torture appointments. *They can always torture me tomorrow.*

They wandered the new subdivisions of the damned. The influx was slow enough that Trisha and Becksha had the time to visit all the new souls. They'd be screaming, tortured ironically according to their sins, and Trish and Becksha would leave a gift basket: a jar of locally-sourced honey, rotten fruit, and a note saying, "Welcome to the neighborhood!" A lot of folks called them "the queens of hell."

Hey, they thought, *I could get used to this.*

On Earth, Tony, Tiff, and Jax felt a similar duty to their community. During a committee meeting in Jax's basement, next to his poster for the movie *The Departed,* Tony pulled out the notebook they first used to brainstorm a new religion.

"We gotta make this the best dang dogma," Tony said. "Tell folks *everything* they need to know. We're the real deal! We owe it to them!"

Before, if you asked a scientist, "Hey Chester, how does the world work?" they'd resort to tables, charts, whole generations of journals to explain even the littlest bit. But as Tony, Tiff, and Jax got down to business, they whittled all that down.

Humans are born in sin.

A person is only redeemed by accepting Jesus Christ as their Lord and Savior.

Earthquakes are when God falls down.

With no need for outside references, Tony, Tiff, and Jax answered every quandary, plus a lot of questions nobody was askin. Honest, it made the universe goofy. God had to tweak every equation, personally hold individual water molecules together sometimes. He was working weekends and still couldn't keep up.

The trouble truly started when Nanca Whitmore, a new but devout Crystal Methodist, cornered Tiff one day after service.

"Tiff, you told me about heaven, but what about my dog?"

And Tiff said, "Well what about your dog?"

And Nanca said, "Well I don't think it'd be heaven if Marbles wasn't there."

So Tiff thought about it, and she brought it to the next meeting in Jax's basement.

"Do animals have souls? You know, because you need a soul to get to heaven."

"Well duh," said Tony. He was getting rude with his newfound power.

"I hate to say it," Jax cut in, "but if dogs have souls, wouldn't that mean snakes and warthogs and chimps have souls?"

Everyone groaned—ever since he started talking to God, Jax was becoming a huge bummer.

At first, the inclination was to say, yep, all animals have souls. But then Jax said, "What about mosquitos?" and they realized bugs, too, were technically animals. But not for long. Tony laid it out:

"We gotta draw a line. Pick a feature, let's say spines, and if you got one? Boom, soul, into heaven you go. You don't? Well, God has a spine, and if you don't, you're outta there."

It worked well enough, they decided. Tony licked the tip of the pen and wrote it in the dogma:

All animals with a spine, a spine of the Lord, possess a soul.

Tiff, however, requested the following exceptions: jellyfish, though spineless, should have a soul. Snakes, though spineful, should not. And chimps, though more human than either, were a little too "uncanny valley" to have a soul.

Jax was still stumped.

"But if you don't have a soul, where do you go when you die?" He got inspired. "What if—and hear me out—what if all the pieces that comprise the creature break down. You know, mushrooms and bacteria come in—eat eat eat. Then a dog comes in and finds the mushrooms—eat eat eat. Maybe a bear eats the dog. And every piece that was used for life is absorbed and, like, lives on forever as a part of the whole universe."

No one liked this.

Tony suggested some sort of not-heaven not-hell, but they all agreed that was a little too "Catholic."

Tiff ended it right there:

"Ugh, just send them to hell, ok???"

This was a blow to the chimps in the Cincinnati Zoo. A collective of primates there had begun—well, no other word for it—worshipping a zookeeper named Dekora. Oh, those chimps loved Dekora. She'd come into work to find piles of mango and dead bugs laid by the enclosure door. The chimps used feces and berries to paint icons of her face on the stone walls. Technically, these chimps beat Tony, Tiff and Jax to the punch—the 10,000th religion! But as they could not file for tax exempt status, well ... tough luck, chimps.

When God learned what he had to do, he broke out in stress hives.

"Oh, come on."

He checked the manual, looking for a loophole, but nope. Tough luck, God.

"You fuckers."

First, he had to remove what constituted the chimps' vital soul-ish essence. They ceased dreaming of tools, no longer cared for their offspring, and made no more gentle chimp love. Then he made the amendments for snakes and jellyfish. Snakeowners watched their snakes with dejection—their beloved pets lost their snakey spark. Jellyfish, meanwhile, confounded biologists, acting in new, decidedly unjellyfish ways—seeking isolation, turning back into polyps to avoid the trauma of adulthood, making gentle jellyfish love.

But God couldn't stop there, because the Cincinnati chimps were *also* heretics. Yep: they had to go to instant hell.

"Sorry, chimps," God said as he pressed the hell button.

The entire chimp enclosure burst into flames that summer day. The 268 children of Mount Overlook K-8 screamed as heretic chimps melted bodily into grease fire—the smell was just awful. God had to take a shower. He sat in the water and couldn't stop crying.

In hell, Trisha and Becksha were starting to have fun. Though torture was the name of the game, with the sudden increase in souls, snakes, chimps, books, and trees, there wasn't enough torture to go around. It got crowded, but not too crowded. Hell kinda hit a sweet spot.

There was plenty to hate, sure—the constant fire, the rivers of congealed disease, the plain yogurt—but that just made you tough. Hell residents were proud to endure hell's obstacles. When a pike ripped them a new anus and mouth, or a boulder of maggots crushed their femurs, they'd just shrug and say, "It's a hell thing!" More than anything, they cherished their freedom from the God of Crystal Methodism—they could finally have sex, play cards, and take the Lord's name in vain.

The residents of heaven watched this all happen below, and felt the way folks in Manhattan thought about Brooklyn circa 2001: *it's not fancy, but it's got somethin'*.

Heaven wasn't doing as well with eternity. Just like hell, it now bustled with souls, but this increase in population was not welcome. All the holy delights were now ruined by tourists. Heaven gained a persistent smell of body odor. After enjoying the ultimate expression of delight for so many lifetimes, this minor inconvenience was worse than any torture.

"Do something!" the righteous souls pleaded the Lord.

God tried to even it out. He cast more fire and disease and bitter dairy products into hell, but whatever he added was imperceptible, like peeing in a lake. Heaven and hell, for lack of a better term, made a switcheroo.

That year, Christian music dominated a lackluster Grammys. The Browns won the Super Bowl. The Tonys didn't happen. God found it harder and harder to get out of bed. He'd sit there and stew, wondering, "What's it going to be today?"

The worst for God was the believers. Now that there was one true religion, prayers became actual witchcraft. The sheer volume of prayers on Sundays incapacitated him. He started going bald. Prayers over sports in particular tore him apart. Most of his time was now spent organizing plane departures, grade school test results, and changing elections. He couldn't quit, and he couldn't choose.

"I wish I could kill myself," God said one day.

Only Jax heard. He kept it to himself—he needed the Buffalo Sabers to win.

The clergy moved their offices out of Jax's basement and into a new compound: the Crystal Towers. As the one true religion, they felt it appropriate to stockpile gold, silver, and a fair amount of aluminum. It went to their heads.

Holy power turned Tony into an ass. He convinced himself that power was his birthright. He told everybody. Like, he'd walk into the bank and announce, "I was chosen! It's in my blood! I always knew!"

He commissioned a big fancy hat, started eating grapes. He ditched pants for robes, grew a mustache. He'd spend days laying in bed, drinking communion rum, and never once wondered why it didn't make him drunk anymore.

Tiff's devotion veered into sadism. Condemning people to eternal hell became an easy way to find parking. In a particularly petty streak, she damned all people named Jared, after a bag boy put her fruit in the same bag as raw beef. Hell was filling up.

More than anything, Jax was unhinged. It wasn't healthy to talk to God all the time. The deity was not the loving father he had imagined, but an anxious worm in his ear. The Lord was full of bad news.

"Hey, it's God: I had to kill another soccer team."

"God here, just sent a pacifist to hell."

"Hey. God again. I'm so sorry about this, but my hands are

tied. Dolphins are now fish, and starfish are technically rocks."

Jax learned how every person he met would one day die. He learned which babies were born to cure cancer, and which were born to punish premarital sex. He stopped showering, stopped cutting his hair and nails. The servants of the Crystal Towers heard him pacing all night, growling like a dog and responding to voices no one could hear.

In the White House, President Izzy took to the drink. He had Stella for breakfast, and ended the night on cheap tequila. He had given up science. Basic physics changed so randomly and often that no one could keep up. Satellites kept falling out of orbit with all the fluctuations in gravity. Biologists were just bored—animals had no more mystery. How did the platypus evolve? God said. Why did the dinosaurs die? God said. Chemists were just thankful atoms held together—for now.

Even drinking couldn't blur the pain. Izzy turned his unoccupied brain to a subject he never cared for: theology. He checked out whole sections from the Library of Congress, watched documentaries, read some self-published books. One night, after his twelfth martini, he made a final discovery while it still mattered.

"Oh my dear gosh."

That's right: alcohol no longer made you drunk. Because now *all* alcohol symbolized the blood of Christ, it was stripped of its drunkening power. You see, if you drank blood, even Jesus' blood, it wouldn't get you drunk. So if something *symbolized* that, by the transitive property it technically—heh heh, well, you get the idea.

Izzy didn't care. He had sold his nation, heck, the whole world, to a cruel and vengeful God. If he couldn't get drunk, he'd drink to be sick.

CHAPTER 3: THE END, THE BEGINNING

The reign of Crystal Methodism did end, and nothing Tony, Tiff, or Jax said could stop it. It was all because of that rascal, hell.

Though a metaphysical realm, hell still took up space—God's space. He had basically built the afterlives in his yard: heaven up front with the roses, hell out back with the crabgrass. He liked being able to check outside the window on the eternities, like watching mischievous children. Hearing the moans and groans mix together resulted in a sound not unlike windchimes.

While only a year passed on Earth, an increasing infinity had gone by simultaneously in hell. As more souls and soulless creatures poured into it, second after second, it began to fill up, then fill *way* up.

The pleasant in-between period had passed—hell was starting to feel like hell again. It was too crowded to breathe. Trisha and Becksha couldn't deliver gift baskets. They couldn't move. Though pressed increasingly closer to one another, they couldn't hear their desperate pleas over the clamoring of the damned. They knew a loneliness only the eternal can know.

When Tiff damned every Jason after a Jason rear ended her Sonata, the straw broke that poor camel's back. Yep, all those tortured souls and soulless husks pressed closer, and closer, until they combined, until they *all* combined.

"God dammit," Becksha said, right before she became a single point.

It wasn't just hell. Heaven filled up like a clogged toilet at a football game. The folks there were in true agony as they too became a single point, if you'd believe it. No ma'am, there was no difference between heaven and hell no more. Each became a void where all entered and nothing left. Any refuge of the dead will eventually become a black hole.

As God was cleaning his disposal, he heard the windchime hum of torture and delight go silent. He got a chill. God looked out his kitchen window, and where once he saw the thriving metropolis of hell, he now saw ... nothing at all.

"Gadzooks."

He ran to the front patio, and saw not heaven, but instead felt the growing pull of gravity. He took off his hat.

"Storm's comin."

While God nailed planks over the windows, pressed his furniture against the doors, he thought about Tony, Tiff, and Jax.

If those knuckleheads could have been *a teeny bit* more robust in their afterlife dogma, this could've all been avoided. For all the complexity of the universe, they could only come up with two options. Two wildly different, forever options. It wasn't fair, either: lots of doctors, humanitarians, infants, and animals went to hell for technicalities. The same could be said for all the terrorists, murderers, and skateboarders in heaven. Some folks were really *on the line*, but because of tax hiccups or a stray swear, ended up with an eternity of damnation to their name. At least eternity didn't last long.

A year to the day after Crystal Methodism became the 10,000th religion, the swirling event horizons of heaven and hell overwhelmed the metaphysical space where God resided. Blackholes breached the kitchen, the foyer, the stairs, and the laundry. God hunkered down in the bathroom, afterlives whirring behind the door, cussing so much he could've damned himself.

He knew he had hours, maybe minutes before his own reward and punishment would spaghettify him into God ribbons. He was no match for two such insurmountable forces.

But before he met his grisly end, well, something like a

miracle happened. The metal in his bracelets began to quiver, flex, then crack.

"Oh my me!"

The bracelets blasted apart, constructed of weaker material than God and his bathroom. Despite the storm, God felt waves of relief wash from his toes to his halo. He was free. He wept there, next to the tub.

The tiles of the bathroom began to creak and flex. God drew a bath. The girders warped. He put "The Idiot" by Iggy Pop on the stereo. The roof began to tear off. God sank into the bubbles.

No one remembered to wish him "Happy Birthday."

With a sense of dignity, God took his own life. It felt right to put an end to the whole dang thing. His last words were these:

"Good riddance."

No one heard God's last words. That is, save Jax.

"We might have a problem," he told Tony and Tiff.

As the blackholes consumed God's body, then each other, the three clergy held an emergency, midnight meeting. They tested Jax's hypothesis: they wrote in the notebook. Nothing. They prayed for small, easy things, like clouds and triangles. Nothing. Tony lamented.

"Without God, heaven, or hell, I mean ... our religion just doesn't pack the same punch." He grabbed Jax by the collar of his polo. "You're positive? You can't hear *anything?*"

"Not a word, not a sigh. Nothing."

Tony dropped Jax to the ground. Tiff extended her pinky from a tightly closed fist, and chewed on the nail.

"Maybe we can keep it a secret."

What people noticed first was the lack of hellfire. After a

few accidental "oh my God"s during lovemaking, word got out: yep, you could take the big guy's name in vain again. Then, it was the failure of prayer. The Browns stopped winning games, desperate students failed math exams, the wrong pregnancies took and the right ones didn't. Scientists got back to work, and made a startling discovery.

President Izzy interrupted "The Bachelor" to deliver the news to the nation.

"We aren't sure when, or how, but the evidence is clear: God, our friend, the big dog, has died."

They held a traditional, Crystal Methodist funeral. They buried a symbolic, empty coffin, ate appetizers and cheese balls, then drank. Pretty quickly, they learned the third sign that God was gone: they could get drunk again.

Crystal Methodism remained the national religion, but the believers weren't sure what, if anything, they were supposed to believe. The next Sunday service at the former Dairy Queen earned only $2 million in revenue—a steep dropoff. Tony, Tiff, and Jax knew the end was near.

Tony gratefully succumbed to the drink, as did President Izzy. Tiff felt useless, unable to heal the sick, and moved back in with her mom. Jax alone felt better after God's passing. He could sleep through the night, could meet new people without knowing how they would die. The voice in his head was gone forever.

"Good riddance."

The remaining worldwide network of Crystal Methodist Pastors, Brothers, and Sisters tried to continue the ministry, but motivation was lacking. Forget heaven, forget God—what was the point of a religion without hell? Seminarians in the Crystal Methodist Seminary tried to brainstorm answers, but came up short. Most dropped out, moved back home to Ohio or Michigan. When three of them met in the cafeteria, it was almost empty.

"What do we do now?" asked the Pastor.

"We already had so much training," said the Sister.

"*Useless* training. What can you even do with a religion after God dies?" said the Brother.

They all thought on this point for a long time.

"I mean, you don't necessarily need God for a religion," said the Pastor.

"How?" asked the Brother.

"Yeah," the Sister said, "if there's no God, all a religion does is make people ashamed or afraid for no reason."

"Exactly," said the Pastor.

"Ohhh," the Brother realized, "OHHH."

"But what would we worship?" the Sister asked.

"Whatever's left!" laughed the Brother. "God is gone, but that's not the end of the Story."

That last word, it stirred something in each of them, a small flame they hadn't felt since God's passing.

Somewhere distant, and yet all around, a new god squirmed in fresh life.

Not yet a man.

But a Boy.

The Story Must Be Told

ACKNOWLEDGEMENTS

The Story Must Be Told is a hearty stew sloshing with the loving chunks of many a sweetheart—too many sweethearts to count. We brim with thank-yous, so much we are like to burst:

A single, broad thank you to Sister Callista, Devon Harris, Liturgical Director Carl, and Deacon Adam for their work on The Story Must Be Told podcast and videos.

Multiple thanks to our guests on the podcast, who voice the Stories of the Story with gusto, including Chaplain Jackie Zebrowski, Cardinal Ed Larson, Marcus Parks, Henry Zebrowski, Ben Kissel, Joe Pera, Holden McNeely, Danny Tamberelli, Elliott Friesen, Katie Hartman, Ashley Brooke Roberts, Jake Young, Betsy Winchester Parks, and Jared Logan.

A round of recognition to the Last Podcast Network for hosting our truth, and honoring our good deeds.

A hefty tip of a thick hat to Jarrod Kluk for his duty to our growing fanbase and the Story Discord, as well as to the moderators Kristofferson De, Douglas Strong, and Ryan.

A special dollop of appreciation to all of our patrons on www.patreon.com/tsmbt, whose donations made this possible.

And finally, an oh-you-shouldn't-have of deep admiration to Sam, Sami Jo, Maggie, Katherine Monasterio, Pete Dawson Barr, Steve "the Penitent" O'Brien, and of course, last but far from least: Chalmsberry "the Boy" Grib.

Seasons of the Story

ABOUT THE AUTHOR

The Story was never born and will never die. Listen to the Story's body of work on The Story Must Be Told podcast—a surreal short fiction anthology hosted by Brother Reid and Pastor Andrew, accompanied by Sister Callista and Devon. Each episode features an original score by Liturgical Director Carl, with editing and sound design by Deacon Adam. It can be found on Soundcloud, Spotify, the Podcasts app, or anywhere else you tune in to grease down.

If you swallowed every word of this book, and would like some gooey greasy poetry to help wash it down, buy **PSALMS 1** of the Story Must Be Told, available at thestorymustbetold.com.

Grease upon you.

thestorymustbetold.com
Twitter and Instagram: @tsmbtpod

For more of Sishir Bommakanti's artwork,
visit www.sishir.com, or Instagram @cadmiumcoffee

Printed in Great Britain
by Amazon